Dorek

Dorek

deaf and unheard

Patricia Borlenghi

Patrician Press
Manningtree

Published by Patrician Press 2015.
For more information: www.patricianpress.com

British Library Cataloguing in Publication Data. A catalogue
record for this book is available from the British Library.

ISBN paperback edition 978-0-9930106-0-6 e-book edition
978-0-9930106-1-3

Printed and bound in Peterborough by Printondemand-
worldwide

http://www.patricianpress.com

Patricia Borlenghi set up the Patrician Press at the end of 2012 after completing her MA in Creative Writing. She is the author of several children's books including *Chaucer the Cat and the Animal Pilgrims, Dear Aunty* and *The Bloomsbury Nursery Treasury,* and has worked in publishing throughout her career. She now divides her time between England and Italy. *Dorek* is the last title in her trilogy. The other titles are *Clarisse* and *Zaira.*

Review for *Zaira*

'Patricia Borlenghi tells the story of this ménage a trois with sensitivity and verve, allowing us to glimpse the complex emotions and destinies that have linked these three so inextricably. Readers will delight in the author's occasional use of dialect, her references to food and festive traditions drawn from one of Italy's great culinary capitals and in the detailed attention to period setting which all make this book come irresistibly alive' **Linda Lappin**, author of *The Etruscan, Katherine's Wish*, and *Signatures in Stone*.

For C. J.

Many thanks to Dr Mark A. Carrigan, John Dickie, Danielle Fitzgerald, Verina Jones, Jim Murray, Sandra Kramer, Jan Turner, and of course, to Charlie Johnson.

Thanks to Tim Roberts for his "Magnox (Pattern Paper)" lino-cut print for the cover illustration.

Please note that the text contains some deliberate 'hearing impaired' mistakes.

"Then, with that faint, fleeting smile playing about his lips, he faced the firing squad; erect and motionless, proud and disdainful, Walter Mitty the Undefeated, inscrutable to the last."

James Thurber *The Secret Life of Walter Mitty.* 1939

Deafness is a disability which is not taken seriously enough.

Personally, being deaf has never disabled nor hindered me.

It hasn't affected my ability to think and to write.

Everyone has a novel in them, they say.

This is not a romance, no boy meets girl stuff.

Finding that journal is what triggered this need in me.

How many people have this urge to write?

Millions I guess.

How many books are there to read?

Billions...

Quite easy now to publish, so I will and be damned.

My Side of the Fence

A very different person
Inside an indifferent body.
I imagine adventures,
Indulge in fantasies,
Without making the leap.
Unassuming, pale and listless
I thrust out my chest,
Pump up my muscles,
And punch Michael Gove...
I have lots of things to
Shout from the rooftops but I don't.
I could argue my case, come up with solutions
Yet no one would listen...

It was February 2011 when I went into the city of Christchurch. I could see the devastation, all the badly damaged buildings. There was nothing left of the Copthorne, no reception, area, no windows, nothing, all rubble. It reminded me of the bomb sites in London when I was young. It was hard walking over the tumbled down concrete. The hotel didn't have to be completely demolished but it would take years to rebuild it. I was lucky I was staying in a camp site outside the city and although it was very frightening as if gravity was suspended, nothing much in my van was broken, as everything was plastic and secured in place. I remember time stopped still and the noise was deafening, even for me. I felt that I was being whirled round in one of those horrid fairground waltzers. Fortunately it didn't last that long, although I felt like being sick afterwards.

That journal belonged to *her*. She left it in the van! I didn't know what I should do with it so I thought I could ask the Copthorne to forward it to her in case she needed it urgently. Fat chance. There was no way I could leave a journal there, there was nowhere to leave anything anywhere. I didn't want to keep something that belonged to her. It was too personal. Then I changed my mind. I could give it back to her in England. She must have dropped it when she got out at the airport. She was in such a state when she said goodbye. She told me she still hadn't managed to cancel her booking. I volunteered to call into the hotel myself the following day (rather than use the telephone) to cancel the room but that's when the earthquake happened.

I read the journal from start to finish in the van the night I was camping in Nelson. There was one page missing, right at the back. It must have detached itself – the pages were perforated – and dropped out somewhere. Her writing wasn't that impressive. Her poems are just as weak as mine, her acronyms of towns corny. It was like a rather boring travelogue.

Now I want to put the record straight. Write my memoir, or rather my ramblings; let's call it the *Diary of a Nobody* like that other chappie's. I am a nobody and try not to take myself too seriously, a a self-effacing type, living on the periphery of society. The solitary occupation of writing is appealing. I try not to dwell on my being deaf. Shutting myself away from the world helps me concentrate. There are no distractions, as I can't hear them.

Let's start at the beginning

I was born Dorek Piotr Wiadrowski. I never thought I was abnormal. As I grew older other boys, teenaged boys, thought they were different, anguished, filled with despair. I didn't, not realising I couldn't hear very well. I lip-read intuitively, always having to face a person to hear them. Rosa didn't notice this straight away. She was more concerned that I read holding a book too closely. It turned out my eyesight was odd, short-sighted in my left eye and long-sighted and astigmatic in my right. My right eye has a slight squint even now. Never bad enough to be operated on but I did wear a patch over one eye for a while and when I started wearing glasses the left lens was covered in Elastoplast. A couple of other boys had the same problem, so it never worried me. I have a bunion on my left foot, always have done, ever since I was a nipper. When I looked at other children's straight feet I thought they were weird and should have had crooked feet like mine.

It was a shock when I discovered I wasn't normal. I've never achieved anything with my life. I bumble along but I have an optimistic streak, don't really worry about anything. I believe someday something good will happen to me or I will perform some extraordinary act of kindness. I never feel depressed. This could be genetic. The Italian side of my family, my uncles and cousins were always very jolly. Even Rosa, my mother, often tried to put on her sunny face. Some people I know are more predisposed to be depressed, bipolar, have nervous breakdowns, whatever. Maybe I am lucky to be so phlegmatic; I don't feel things too deeply. I'm interested in things: animal rights, philosophy, politics, but I take everything in my stride. Like when I fell out of that window onto a car. My life stopped still. I definitely had a strange sensation of seeing dazzling yellow light at the end of the proverbial tunnel, an out of body experience and all that. Yet when I woke up from the coma after eight days, it was as if nothing had happened. I was so numb and blank, I accepted the experience. Admittedly I have fantasies. Always have. The Walter Mitty of my generation. I hope what I'm writing isn't libellous or else I could end up getting scuppered, sued even, by our respected establishment. One of the things to check before publication I suppose. And even the great Hilary Mantel got stick for writing what I thought was a perfectly innocuous story, *The Assassination of Margaret Thatcher*. Watch out, the thought police are about.

Today I shot the Mayor of London

A puzzling character, I have never understood his popularity. Under that lavish blond hair, cuddly, humorous demeanour and slightly rumpled persona lurks a menacing and sinister man. He seems affable but he is a hard-centred chocolate. He's certainly not interested in helping the disadvantaged or unemployed. His vision for London is constructed on high finance and big profits. Anyway he was on a photo-shoot riding a Borish bike. And apparently they won't be Barclays-sponsored for much longer. I shot him with my silver pistol. Then I hopped on the same bike and cycled to the House of Commons. It was a Wednesday, during Question Time. I managed to get past the security checks, greasing the guards' palms with a wad of notes, and took my seat in the visitors' gallery. From there I carefully aimed a shot at our Prime Minister. Unfortunately, the pistol jammed and I was herded down to face Black Rod, who promptly kneed me in the groin and hit me with his Rod.

I can see the Daily Hate headlines:

Shirker kills Mayor then takes shot at PM! Blame the welfare state!

Then again it most probably wouldn't be a good idea to make a martyr out of Borish. The government would use this as an excuse to abandon the welfare state completely. I just wrote warfare state… not sure if this is connected to my deafness or just word confusion.

We can't all be privileged, go to Eton. We aren't all capable of finding a good job. Without a safety net, there would be more crime, more atrocities, more chaos. My opinions are ignored and like me, no one ever does anything to halt this tide of bigotry and nastiness. We sink back in our apathy. Writing down my political philosophy assuages my guilt, a little.

Sometimes I feel an exploding anger, as if I'm in an electrified chair or I'm about to spontaneously combust. This is an odd sensation, as usually I'm ultra-calm. I don't understand why I get urges to kill, or perhaps just to shock, get myself into the newspapers, be famous at long last. I don't suppose I ever will. If I purchased a knife or a gun, or made a bomb, I doubt I could actually commit murder. I'm too cowardly. I can imagine these things but I would never have the courage to carry them out, just as I could never slash my wrists in the bath and end it all. But the fact is, I can think these things and my thoughts can't harm people, whatever the Catholic Church preaches…

I'm still digressing. I said I would start at the beginning. Write things the way I see them, not like *her*.

Dorset Street

Never bleak,
Always cheerful.
I like my solitary,
Silent world.
My childhood memories
Do not make me cry.
I am however nostalgic
For my bare knees,
Those bald-headed faces,
Eyeless and earless.
Dressing them in imaginary hats
With my flannel or plastic toys.
Making them wear glasses
With my ringed fingers.
In the dank, boiling, peeling bathroom,
Water steaming from the old geyser,
Every Saturday,
On bath night.

I was born on 9 April 1949. Possibly this is the reason I like neat, consecutive or sequential numbers. Arithmetic I find easy to do and can't understand why others don't:
  7+7 divide by 7 + 7 x 7 – 7 = 56! Easy peasy.

11/12/13 is a good example of a 'neat' date. It contains the last consecutive numbers of this century.

I am also a very accomplished cricket scorer, even though I was never a great cricketer. I was always the first at school to volunteer to keep the score. I loved the way every section has to cross-tally and add up, rather like keeping accounts. Damien and me used to play the *Book Cricket Game*. We got the idea from the *Eagle* comic. A page from a textbook was chosen at random and each letter or symbol was counted according to a formula. The scorecard looked amazingly realistic with many of the innings scoring up to 300. Problem is, after all this time I can't remember the formula. I asked Damien, as I thought he would know but he denied all knowledge of the book game and said we used to play the game with a six-sided pencil. Odd how we remember things differently. I thought the formula was to do with a letter equalling the number of runs scored. Sometimes I played it on my own. I do wonder if I have a mild form of Asperger's.

I grew up in Dorset Street, Islington, near the Angel. I suppose it was a privileged place to live. A bus ride away from the West End, cinemas, galleries, museums, theatres. I remember seeing the Collins Music Hall on Islington Green when I was a toddler, but I was too young to go there. There was also a long arcade at the Angel where the parents of that guy now on TV had a pram shop. Well, the dad did. His mum was Sheree Winton, a minor starlet. She was known as the English Jayne Mansfield. I remember Jayne too. She came to the Angel once and I climbed up onto her Rolls Royce and was promptly pulled off by her chauffeur. Sadly, they both came to sticky ends, Sheree committing suicide and Jayne being decapitated in a car crash.

When Rosa finally realised I had a hearing problem in my teens she sent me to Dr Linley, the doctor at the end of the road. She had a mannish appearance with short hair and very bushy eyebrows. She wore a tailored shirt and a tweed jacket, accompanied by a pencil-thin skirt, exposing her slim legs and narrow ankles in black high heels. Odd combination.

At a couple of London hospitals I endured several hearing tests as well as brain scans, electrodes to the brain and even mental arithmetic, counting in thirteens or seventeens backwards (this was pure torture as the technician kept shouting, 'faster, faster'), to test my balance and several blood tests. I was ultimately diagnosed with otosclerosis, a hereditary hearing disease. It affects more women than men. Rosa couldn't think of anyone in her family who was deaf.

'Well, it must be your father's side.'

(Otosclerosis usually affects both ears and the ear bones gradually fuse together. The hearing loss in both ears is usually uniform but my right ear is slightly worse than my left one. When I lie on my right ear at night I can hear beeps, like the tweeting of birds or signals from transmitters. It could be some sort of code – someone trying to communicate with me, but I have no idea who.)

I had NHS hearing aids fitted at the Ear Nose and Throat Hospital near King's Cross. It was the sixties when long hair on boys was becoming fashionable so I grew my hair long to cover my ears. No one noticed the cumbersome hearing aids, unless I pushed my hair back behind my ears, so I tried to remember not to do this. Sometimes, to show I'm non-hearing I do point to my aids as some people think I'm thick rather than deaf. I am aware people can be unsympathetic and trivialise it but I have grown accustomed to this. And the semi-silence rather than roaring noises can be comforting.

'Stop shouting!' Rosa would say.

'I can't help it, I'm deaf. I don't know I'm shouting. I just wanted to say it's hard to keep the hearing aids in. I want to pull them out all the time.'

'Well, you are shouting, just keep it down a bit. The audiologist at the hospital said it would take a while for you to get used to them. You have to persevere. It's not like wearing your glasses that you take off and put on as you like. You have to keep them in all the time.'

'Not when I'm in bed though,' I deliberately muttered.

We lived on the first floor of a Georgian house. It belonged to the priests from St Stanislaus Polish church on the corner of our road. The three priests lived in the house next to the church, the presbytery, but they had bought the house we lived in for their Polish language school. The house comprised a basement, ground floor and two upper floors. The basement was used for storage. The Polish language school was held every Saturday morning in the two rooms on the ground floor. The place was very quiet the rest of the week but when all the kids arrived it was pandemonium, like Battersea Funfair. They were all shouting and screaming and running around before classes began. When Father Jonas from the church rang the bell for class to start, they all became miraculously silent and well behaved. Rosa made me attend the junior class but occasionally I managed to get out of it. I said I wasn't feeling well and needed to rest after being at my other school for the rest of the week. Later I'd say I had football practice or an actual game.

I never learnt much Polish. Just a few things such as:

Cześć – hello. It can also mean goodbye, like '*ciao*' in Italian.

Dziękuję – thank you.

Tak is yes. *Nie* is no or not.

What I always say is: *Nie mówię po polsku*. I don't speak Polish or *Nie rozumiem*. I don't understand.

The two other things I remember are: '*Tutaj jest książka*'. Here is a book and '*Tu jest krzesło*'. Here is a chair.

What I enjoyed as a kid was running through the basement. There were two rough wooden doors with bolts on each side of the back extensions of the house, leading to the garden. One door was at the end of the corridor, opposite a dilapidated toilet with a large wooden seat and a box for flimsy sheets of Izal toilet paper, and the other was in a brick wash-house leading from the storage room. I would unbolt both doors, run round through the back room, dodging all the boxes and back through the other side tens of times, and then run out to the garden which the Mad Priest tended. I used to hunt for treasures in the bare earth or play tennis with bats from the storeroom but without a net, or my personalised version of cricket with the Mad Priest. I dictated the rules and always won and he never cared. He used to guffaw hoarsely when I beat him and just seemed happy to play with me. He lived on the top floor in an open-plan studio with a little bathroom in the ceiling space at the top of the stairs. The layout of our flat was different with a kitchen/living room overlooking the garden and a front bedroom with two full-length windows. Our bathroom was on the lower mezzanine floor. When I was seven, Rosa divided our bedroom into two (with one window in each room) and she slept on a divan/sofa bed in what became the sitting room. My new bedroom was small but I loved it. I chose the orange floral curtains and orange-striped wallpaper. I played with my second-hand Meccano set and tin soldiers my cousins had given me, and I had a rag doll called Beryl which I used to beat mercilessly.

Rosa and I often misunderstood each other but that could have been because of my hearing loss; when I couldn't hear the words, I guessed their sequence.

Rosa: 'I have work to do.'

'You have to go for a walk?'

'No, I said I have much to do.'

'You must do what?'

'You, though, must think things through. You mustn't guess.'

'What did you say then, that I know things? Nah, I don't.'

Rosa mentioned a few times that the Polish priests were threatening to put up the rent which she couldn't afford. She said this was an excuse to evict us.

'They've set the date for the rent increase.'

'They've sent what for the rent, where?'

I didn't understand and I didn't care.

The Mad Priest looked after me when I was little while Rosa was working at the hospital. He took me to school and back until I was able to walk there on my own. It wasn't far. He didn't speak much English. He always wore black and a tall fedora hat, and when he left the house even I could hear the noise he made. I could glimpse him from my front window always running back several times to make sure he had shut the door properly. The front door was covered with hardboard and painted a nondescript shitty mid-brown, unlike *hers* across the road, which had been stripped back to the original Georgian door –although strangely, painted a banana-yellow.

Sometimes he'd rush up the stairs into his spotless kitchen to see if he'd left the gas or electricity on. He used to ask me to check all the gas rings and electric switches when he left me on my own in the house. So I used to run up from our flat into his immaculately tidy kitchen area, test all the switches and knobs were turned off and yell at him at the top of my voice:

'ALLE IST KLAR!'

In Polish, it's '*wszystko jest jasne*' but I could never remember how to pronounce it. I had seen a subtitled film about World War Two on the telly. The Germans were giving the all clear and I've never forgotten these words. When I was in his flat I imagined that I was a soldier checking the distance between the enemy line and my camp with a mine detector or making sure there no bombs that could be detonated.

I remember words like that from when I could hear better.

I often sat at our yellow Formica kitchen table to do my homework. Out of the window I could see the slate roof of the extension/conservatory on the ground floor, part of the Polish school. I regularly spied wood pigeons and the occasional blue tit perched on the roof and one day a splendid green woodpecker with his red head and Batman mask around his staring eyes. The delightfully vivid colours in contrast to the grey slate made a deep impression on me. He looked at me very briefly and then turned around, intent on something else. Who would have thought it in the heart of London? I only saw him the once, never again. Did I imagine that too?

There was a dream or fantasy I had about Princess Anne being kidnapped outside the Polish church and it was me who intervened and rescued her. I managed to beat off the kidnappers with my sword and I was awarded the George Cross at Buckingham Palace for my heroic deeds.

Much later, when I was just about to move out of Dorset Street, I dreamt that the Polish Pope John Paul II visited the church and, as one of his Swiss bodyguards, I was beating off people trying to touch him. (In fact he visited the church much later, in 1982.)

One of my earliest memories is that as a baby I was looked after by Scotch Mary, or Mary Stewart as she was really called. She was plump and rosy and lived next door, the other side to Susan. Scotch Mary had a daughter called Teresa and a son called Billy. She was married to a Maltese who never spoke. Scotch Mary did enough talking for both of them. When I was two, I fell out of my pushchair when Scotch Mary was wheeling me to the baker's or the grocer's two streets away. I tried to stand up, wobbled and fell out the side. I started crying and she yelled at me to stop, so I did...

'Stop yerr fussing now, it's only a wee bump on yerr heed...wee boys shouldna cry.' (But I'm no good at Scottish accents.) They moved when I was about four or five.

Mrs Bradshaw reminded me of Scotch Mary. She ran the boarding house we went to once in Scarborough. I know we had Yorkshire pudding on a separate plate and Rosa always stirred the batter with a knife after that, as taught by Mrs Bradshaw. I can also picture hutches in the back garden, filled with fluffy white rabbits. Me and a girl staying there were allowed to take them out and play with them. They were so soft and cuddly. The girl was horrid though. She had buckteeth and made fun of my name, calling me 'Do-Do', but luckily it never stuck. In Yorkshire I can picture the sandalled feet of the flat-footed stout women I spied out of my pushchair. Another memory is of having measles and chicken pox together, lying in Rosa's bed in the dark and Uncle Franco buying me a red and yellow telephone. I wasn't allowed to read or get out of bed. I loved that phone and played with it until I was eleven. I also remember falling off the hobby-horse in Highbury Fields. My cousin, Uncle Franco's son, took me there. Uncle Franco felt guilty that his son, also called Franco, hadn't been looking after me properly so he bought me a toy. It was a white and black poodle made from looped-wool. I christened it Fifi.

As Rosa was a full-time nurse, she often worked night shifts so Scotch Mary and then the Mad Priest used to put me to bed and I made them read me stories. I don't think Scotch Mary ever read to her own children and raced through reading them as fast as she could but the Mad Priest loved it. It was good for practising his English too.

When Rosa was at home she lavished me with attention, bought me books and toys and cooked my favourite foods.

One of my all-time favourites was chocolate éclairs. Rosa whipped them up like magic. She used a tin nozzle attached to a plastic bag to squeeze out the choux pastry she cooked from the melted butter, flour, beaten eggs, maybe some water, in a little saucepan. After baking them in our prehistoric black and grey-dotted enamel gas cooker she filled them with double cream and topped them with melted dark chocolate in what seemed no time at all. Rosa told me that this pastry had been invented by Catherine de Medici in 1533. When I was watching the *Hairy Bikers* they said it was invented by a French chef more recently, but maybe they were talking about profiteroles, as they said the chef likened them to little '*choux*' or cabbages.

'Do you want another, darling?'

'Do I want a mother? I have you, darling!'

This became a standing joke and we said it to each other all the time.

Rosa and I loved each other, of course, but living in such close proximity to her drove me nuts sometimes, especially as I got older, so it was good to escape into my bedroom and lock the door. She encouraged me to attend the Polish church on Sundays but never came with me. Instead, I used to see *her* there.

I must have been about twelve when I realised I was sexually confused. Part of me wanted to be *her*. I didn't want to kiss her passionately or even 'love' her. I just wanted to look at her. I watched Clarrie, as I called her, from my bedroom window all the time. Her family, called the Villeneuves, who were French, lived opposite us. Sometimes I could spy her inside standing at the window but usually I only saw her leave or enter the front door. The houses on that side of the street were slightly grander and had three steps leading up to the front door; some even had porches. Ours only had one step. The gardens on that side were longer too.

The street had grown dilapidated because of the war but was now becoming more gentrified. In the fifties there were very few cars in the street, which left room for the milk floats, the Corona lorry that delivered soft drinks, the shellfish van selling cockles, prawns, whelks and winkles and the Express ice cream man on his tricycle. The vanilla ice cream was packed in little square green and white cartons, before the advent of ice cream wafers and cornets.

As well as the Polish church there was an Anglican church on the other corner on our side of the street. It eventually got turned into apartments, as did the pub on the corner on her side. Clarrie's house had always been a family house and she, her parents and her grandma had their kitchen and dining room in the basement, an extensive sitting room on the ground floor, four bedrooms on the other floors and at least two bathrooms on one or other of the floors. Many of the other houses in the street had been rented out as one or two-roomed lodgings but eventually others were being renovated and turned back into family houses.

Rosa often said if we'd had the money we could have snapped one up for £500 when I was a baby but she couldn't raise the cash. That must have been when she'd rowed with her brothers who nevertheless weren't interested in acquiring shabby property in Dorset Street. I wonder if they ever regretted that. They're going for over two million. The street is unrecognisable now, all the Georgian features lovingly restored, trees lining the pavements, parking meters and residential permits for the tons of cars parked in every space. The only place that hasn't changed much is St Stan's, the Polish church, and the priests do still own two houses in the street.

Clarrie certainly gave me the impression of looking down on us lowly fellow residents, with her exaggerated airs and graces. She looked like a doll with her bright china-blue eyes and her long dark perfect ringlets, always dressed in smock dresses with white Peter Pan collars. In winter she wore a grey-blue speckled tweed waisted coat with navy-blue velvet collar, sometimes with matching navy-blue velvet beret. She often wore white lacy socks and black patent shoes strapped with button fasteners high around her delicate ankles. When she was going to a party or dressed up for some special occasion she wore powder-blue or white organdie dresses and immaculately whitened open-toe sandals, exposing her bare ankles. I used the same whitening for my canvas tennis shoes but mine never looked as white.

Rosa knew Celeste, her grandmother, and popped over to see her occasionally. Celeste had saved me as a baby. I caught pneumonia and nearly died. Rosa had panicked, briefly forgetting all her nursing training, and had rushed across the road with me to use their telephone, as we didn't have one then. Celeste warmed me at an open fire in her basement living room, rubbing my hands and feet which had turned blue, breathing life back into my screeching mouth.

Rosie, as she was called by neighbours, kept herself to herself and we never mixed socially with the Villeneuves but she always gave Celeste a box of Black Magic chocolates at Christmas. I resented it. I wanted them for myself.

Clarrie must have heard the story of her grandmother saving me but she pretends I don't exist. She is so snooty, not just with me, and never plays with any children in the street.

I loved that blue organdie with printed flowers she wore for her seventh birthday party. I can't remember if I was actually invited; whether this is a true memory or a fantasy. I often have this problem, especially about Clarrie. Sometimes, going back, I realise the intensity I experience comes from the memories I have of her and not from her as an actual person.

This is what I remember about her party: there were only three boys there, André, Renzo, the Italian boy in Dorset Street who became a hairdresser, and me. André was Belgian and his mum knew Clarrie's mum, Delphine.

(Years later when we were at the same wedding reception for an Italian couple we both knew, Renzo, silly idiot, confessed he told Clarrie I fancied her. I never forgave him. He got his comeuppance and I got my sweet revenge. Although I always thought Renzo was gay, he married a French woman called Chantelle and soon after I saw him at that wedding they moved to Fort Worth, Texas, where he opened up a hairdressing salon. They had a daughter and Renzo became a pillar of the community and very interested in education. Next thing I knew was Mungo or Walter Danesi telling me Renzo was splashed across the centre pages of the *Sun* or *Daily Mirror*. He had divorced Chantelle and remarried. His second wife shot him in a crime of fashion, I mean passion. The details are sketchy and although I googled him just now, it just mentions his premature death, aged forty-nine, but nothing about any murder.)

At her party, Clarrie boasted that her dad was a famous TV actor but when I told Rosa about it she said he had only ever acted on stage and was once given a tiny part in an Armchair Theatre production as a favour by one of his customers at the French restaurant where he worked very long hours. Rosa said she was quite often woken up by the taxi bringing him home, blind drunk. Luckily I never heard any taxi…

My party present was a blue and white plastic sailing boat which had cascaded out of the giant sky-blue and silver-edged crepe paper cracker suspended from their sitting room ceiling. It had been released and pulled open at both ends by

Delphine and Celeste. Then we children had to catch one toy. Clarrie got the wind-up fairy godmother.

I loved that boat and used to play with it in my bath all the time after that, along with my black and white wooden tug and my plastic yellow duck, so it must be true.

I did know a few kids in the street. I 'played out' with them, as we used to say, but Clarrie never 'played out'. Susan lived next door to me, the other side to Scotch Mary, and she taught me to ride a bike. She showed me her private parts once when we were sitting on her freshly whitened doorstep. Red and moist, mysterious looking flaps and openings, all unknown and unexplored and better for it, I thought. Her uncle 'Fluff' was weird; I'm not sure if he was a relative or not. He was always pawing her. Nowadays he would definitely be classed as a paedophlle.

My other friend was Steven 'I'll be Queen'. He was obviously gay but we didn't think anything of it. His idea of bean, I mean being, Queen was to wrap a white flannelette sheet around himself which looked extremely silly. My usual role was either as the cool cowboy or a Red Indian (that's what we called Native Americans in those days!) depending on who were the goodies or the baddies that day. I always felt more sympathetic to the 'Red Indians'. It was always me who had to rescue Steven. He used to go all floppy and feeble on me when I touched him. I loved him all the same. The poor thing, I discovered years later, died of AIDS. Sydney and Michael were older than me, so we weren't friendly. They had a terrible fight in the street once, punching each other surprisingly hard. The blood really upset me. I couldn't bear it and cried. Alan Cliff, my hero, comforted me. Soon after, Rosa bought me a brand new red scooter and I used to whizz up and down Dorset Street or around the block. Rosa wouldn't let me go any further. One day I fell off in the newly tarred road and cut my knee. I didn't cry but Alan comforted me again. I still have the scar and it always reminds me of him.

Rosa said I was a lucky 'golden baby' to be growing up in the Macmillan 'you've never had it so good' years of the fifties. Hmm, I couldn't agree with that.

St Raphael's

I am in Liverpool Street Station
Going on a school trip
To Our Lady of Walsingham
In Norfolk.
Climbing up to the shrine
On the stony pathway
Is hard and physically gruelling.
Supposedly, spiritually rewarding.
The station is surprisingly empty.
There are alarms going off.
We have to take shelter, lie down.
There has been a suspected attack
By Boston Tea Party
American terrorists.
A bomb has been found.
I lie down against a toilet
Spoiling my school uniform grey shorts.

Rosa wanted me to do well at school, although after I was
diagnosed as deaf her ambitions for me became somewhat
diluted. Before then, when I was four and a half, she sent
me to St Raphael's, a tiny little preparatory convent school in
nearby Douglas Terrace, its public gardens stretching across
the entire terrace into City Road. The half where my school
was had been a bombsite and was converted into an enclosed
garden to match the one on the other side of the terrace leading
to the old Angel tube station. When Rosa and I walked along
through the post-war rubble we used to pretend we were

climbing a mountain and sing, 'I love to go a-wondering long the mountain track' hideously out of tune. Rosa had a good contralto voice. She said with hindsight that it was because of my deafness I couldn't sing in tune but I could hit the right notes if I concentrated enough. I couldn't dance either. No 'sense of rhythm,' screeched the nuns.

The school was next to the St James Catholic church. It consisted of two adjacent five-story Georgian houses. The nuns lived in one house, the ground floor of which was used for cloakrooms, and the other house had been converted into classrooms. We had to wear indoor plimsolls and more than once I found a shiny black beetle inside one of them. The first time I put my foot inside the shoe I felt the beetle's hard body. I always checked after that as I didn't like to crunch their carapaces. The school only had about eighty pupils. I was in a tiny class of nine. So at St Raphael's I had no trouble understanding as everyone who spoke to me was near enough to hear. Perhaps that's why my deafness wasn't detected until later. Each floor had two schoolrooms with dividing doors, kept slightly ajar so we could see the children in the other class.

I was hoping that *she* would come to my school and sit in the younger class in the adjacent room. She never did. She went to some posh girls-only convent in Highbury. She wore a straw boater in summer. The girls at our school wore panama hats. That's how I knew her school was so posh.

At my school one nun taught both classes on each floor so there were only three teaching nuns in all. In my first and second year the teacher was Sister Cordelia. I thought this a pretty name but she wasn't, being tall and scrawny, wearing round thin black-plastic-rimmed glasses and having stubble on her chin. As their nuns' habits covered everything except their faces, I got to know their facial features intimately and she really was as ugly as a fairy-tale witch.

While I'm writing this I wonder why there is so much fuss about Muslim women wearing veils. Nuns and many female peasant farmers cover their heads. Nuns though show more of themselves these days. This is partly to do with fashion or custom, no big deal. And wearing full burka can cover a variety of sins and is a great disguise. Maybe I'll try it one day.

Sister Gladys Mary was the nun in charge of the third and fourth years. I thought Gladys was a strange name for a nun. One day while she was passing I got my finger caught in the door at the top of the steps leading to the Salle. I started to cry. Her fresh pink face covered in ginger down loomed over me and she slapped me round the legs and kept screaming:

'Stop that crying, stop that crying,' in her broad Irish accent.

She and Scotch Mary have stopped me from crying virtually ever since.

On the third floor was Sister Primrose. She was tiny, sweet-looking but demonically fierce. All we ever did in the top class was fill out endless eleven plus exam papers for English, Arithmetic and Intelligence. When I finally did my Arithmetic exam I was puzzling over a problem and Sister Primrose pointed out that I had already worked out the correct answer.

By the time I reached the top class, Sister Cordelia had retired and a very young and glamorous nun took her place. She was called Sister Camilla and wore black kitten heels under her long, disguising, and voluminous black habit. We all thought this was very daring. One day we all sat around, even the boys, discussing fashion and make-up with her. She seemed so vain for a nun. I bet she didn't last long.

The headmistress was Sister Mary Magdalene but we only saw her at assembly or when we had to climb up to her study on the top floor to be chastised. Assembly was held in the huge room, or 'Salle' as it was called, which was in an extension at the back of the ground floor classrooms. We had to line up in rows every morning after mass for assembly. I can't remember what was said – more prayers possibly. The only clear memory is of a boy in my class called Christopher who wet himself standing in line. He was crossing his legs but it was too late. The amber urine trickled down his thighs onto the wooden floorboards.

Alongside was a small playground, which led through a door in its brick walls to another playground belonging to St James Primary School. We were allowed to play there during the midday break. Some of the primary school children jeered at us for going to a 'private' school, but mostly we ignored their jibes and joined in their games without really getting friendly with any of them. And while I was there the fees were only nine guineas a term, which didn't seem that much for a private school.

My school mainly consisted of girls. In my year there was Joan who seemed fidgety and ill at ease. She left under a cloud (amidst rumours of her blowsy mum being a prostitute) and went to a Protestant school instead which was considered worse than a mortal sin in those days. Then there was Italian Stella who said her father was Count Martini, but the rumour was that she was illegitimate. Her mum was unmarried and had been his secretary. Stella said she wanted to be a flamenco dancer when she grew up but all I can visualise is her stomping both her feet up and down like a wooden puppet. Nicole was the closest I had to a proper girlfriend. She loved horses and galloped rather than ran, neighed rather than laughed and told dirty jokes. Sometimes she came to play in the garden at Dorset Street. She built fences from wood she found lying around in the storeroom and jumped over them while I watched her admiringly.

We played football in the small playground at the back. We created one narrow goal at the bottom of the steps leading to a mysterious part of the convent. Fat Carmen was always the goalie. She had this knack of spreading her navy-blue gym slip wide to catch the ball between her legs. She rarely failed, as she didn't even have to move. I liked to see the ball hit the widened pleats of her skirt and never thought of this as cheating.

When I was nine, boys over seven were no longer allowed to attend the school but boys like me were able to stay until the top class. My best friend was Graham, who seemed to be the only true English boy there. There was also a little Tunisian boy called Hubert pronounced with a silent 't', but he didn't stay very long. We boys wore white shirts, navy jerseys and blazers, navy and yellow striped ties and grey shorts and long grey stockings. When the rules about boys changed, the uniform changed to maroon so every parent had to fork out for new clothes. Rosa happily bought me the new blazer and tie but made me wear the same grey shorts, which got skimpier and skimpier as I neared the age of eleven. And in winter my knees were always frozen red, with sandpapered-looking skin and dried-up scabs.

I started going to the local library on my own, or with Graham or Nicole, when I was ten. I loved books about Captain Hornblower and Sherlock Holmes and read all of them but *Riddle of the Sands* by Erskine Childers was my favourite. It's a very patriotic spy story written before the First World War and set somewhere on the east coast, but I wasn't sure where.

Rosa was worried about how little I ate at school and Miss Dellarobbia, the lay gym teacher at St Raphael's, called me 'a bag of bones'. Before school Rosa gave me eggnog in a glass tumbler. It was made with one egg yolk, a drop of Marsala and half an eggshell full of sugar. She separated the egg by pouring the white from one half shell to the other until the yolk was left. Early every morning she forced it down my throat. Her other favourite trick was rubbing a clove of garlic on my feet when I developed a fever as I used to spit out all prescribed medicines. It did seem to lower my temperature. Rosa was right about garlic; it is a natural antibiotic. Maybe that's why I love it so much now and put garlic into virtually every meal I make.

We didn't have conventional school meals. The food was delivered from *The Blue Kettle*, a shabby looking café at the Angel which later closed down when the area was revamped. It was situated in the courtyard just after the Empire Cinema (we had five cinemas in those days) and before the junction with City Road. There was a blue tin kettle hanging on a chain at the start of the alley leading to the courtyard. Usually the food was so disgusting I could never eat it: burnt scrambled egg, lumpy pink custard we called Windolene, mashed potato with hard grey bits in it, colourless chewy meat and tinned carrots. The only thing I ever finished eating was some shepherd's pie – a big portion meant for a senior, a much larger boy. There was a diabetic girl in the class above me called Denise whose mother helped out at lunchtimes in the big Salle. I couldn't understand why her mother fed her chocolate éclairs while we had to make do with stodgy puddings and lumpy custard. And this was before the time of 'Thatcher the Milk Snatcher' when, in every school, quarter-pints of milk were kept by the radiators to keep warm. They were not at all pleasant to drink and tepid milk still makes me feel sick. I also have vague memories of bottled orange juice with blue aluminium tops, tablespoons of cod liver oil or malt in dark glass jars, and Ovaltine tablets wrapped in greaseproof paper, which were then superseded by Halibut Orange tablets. We all had to help with the washing up by putting the rinsed cutlery into earthenware jars but Denise was exempted from this, which I found very annoying.

Grammar and spelling were drummed into me at primary school. I don't think of myself as a professional writer but I think I can write just as well as many mediocre writers I have read, especially the young ones who were never taught the basics.

The nuns made us look at maps of the world which we had to trace and copy. The pink parts were the British Empire and seemed to cover quite large areas of the world. The nuns liked to boast that many of these areas were where missionaries had converted the indigenous population to Catholicism. Umm – religion, a very good excuse for political conquest.

Even at that young age, I never understood why Brits were proud of their imperial history, yet resentful of immigrants living here. It seems that it was acceptable for the Brits to invade, destroy and colonise countries in Africa, Asia and elsewhere but not okay for the colonised to obtain British passports to come here.

I made my holy communion and confirmation at St James church, next to my school and then we had a 'breakfast' in the Salle. I remember Rosa crying at the holy communion service. There is a photo of me looking very pious, hands outstretched in prayer, clasping white rosary beads, yet I never really believed in any of it. My blond hair is cut 'short back and sides' and I'm wearing my customary white shirt, striped blue and yellow tie and grey shorts.

Before making my first holy communion I had to make my first confession. I always despised having to 'confess my sins' in those ugly wooden boxes, like upright coffins, which you entered through a door with a small latticed opaque glass window. Then you had to kneel uncomfortably to talk to an invisible priest behind a grate.

'Bless me Father for I have sinned.'

'It has been one week; two weeks; one month; five months since my last confession…' I repeated endlessly until I never went again.

My sins were always the same. I told lies, I was disobedient, I answered my mother back. And that was it. Some boys I knew said the priests were quite probing and asked if they ever had impure thoughts, but no one ever asked me and I never volunteered anything about any impurities.

I would like you to touch me up please, Father, and I will suck your knob, Father.

The priests hearing my confession seemed just as bored as I was. They always mumbled the same penance. I never heard what they said that well but I guessed it was one *Our Father*, and three *Hail Marys*. When I left the confessional, I always did recite the penance, just in case.

For my confirmation, I chose the name Vincent. My Uncle Vince was very pleased but it wasn't because of him. It was Saint Vincent de Paul, a French priest dedicated to serving the poor. I discovered quite recently that you don't get a confirmation name in Italy or in Spanish- or French-speaking countries, only in English-speaking ones. Confirmation is like a baptism and you have to have a godparent.so to add to the myth I chose Uncle Vince. I think Uncle Franco was rather miffed as he was actually closer to me than Vince. I suppose

I should have chosen both, as they were identical twins. It would have been a laugh, but no one else had two godparents so I didn't feel I could do this. I have never used the name Vincent since but apparently confirmation names are legally recognised. Dorek Piotr Vincent Wiadrowski – even more of a mouthful.

Dreaming of being a woman

Last night after I finished writing this, I dreamt I was a woman and I was walking outside in the street completely naked. This was something I used to dream many times as a youth, no clothes on and an enormous erection. I was always embarrassed then, but this time there was a touch of insouciance to my nakedness, even brazenness. How strange, as in real life I am very shy about my body. I was attending some kind of public function, which then turned into a job interview, so I quickly tried to cover my nakedness. I slung a big bag over my bottom and one over my front to cover both my pudenda and my perky, sticking-out breasts. The man who was interviewing me remarked on how much shopping I had done!

Rosa

Bathing in words
I see words
I read words
I write words
Floating slightly above my head, words
Like hundreds of thousands of birds
Squawking seagulls
Piercing and battering my brain.
Yet I cannot hear words
I can remember them
Imagine them
Mispronounce them.
Guess them as in a puzzle.
Italian words where every
Syllable is pronounced,
Easier to understand than
English vocabulary.
Thwarted ambitions,
Words never used,
Forgotten
Or hidden.
What makes us different?
I cannot hear.
Silence
I cannot bear.
Equipment helps
Yet still distorts,
Sounds running away,
Going astray,

Becoming gobbled, swallowed,
Indistinct,
Indistinguishable,
Amongst
Background noises,
Tumbling down.
Words confused,
Fading fast.

My mother, full name, Rosanna Livia Crespi, worked at the French Hospital in Shaftesbury Avenue. And although she worked long hours and didn't spend that much time with me, the general opinion was that she and I were very close. Too close, I suppose. In a way, I wasn't a 'mummy's boy' because she couldn't bear the idea of being called mother or mum so I always called her Rosa. She was secretly pleased that I wasn't the kind of boy who was interested in marriage and children. The idea of being called granny or nana terrified her. She was anxious to keep her youthful figure and not grow old.

She didn't wear much make-up: just a little rouge she kept in a circular white cardboard box trimmed with black; mascara in a pink plastic oblong box fitted with a mirror and a little black brush; and a pale pink lipstick. I was always fascinated by the way she applied her mascara. She used to take out the little brush from the plastic box, spit onto it and then combine the spit with the hard black paste. She then meticulously applied layers of the mascara to her long eyelashes. She was quite vain even though she usually wore tortoiseshell-rimmed glasses and a headscarf. There are photos of her when she was young and she is sultry and beautiful. She once said a writer, a patient of hers, dedicated one of his novels to 'the beautiful Rosa' but I have never found this book.

She admitted to her vanity and often admired her own smooth, young-looking skin but she wore few physical adornments; only a gold cocktail watch and a large diamond ring on special occasions. She had pierced ears (as did most Italian women) and wore either very small pearl or gold studs; never any nail varnish, being a nurse I suppose. I didn't inherit her colouring, as she was olive-skinned with brown hair. But like her, I have good skin and not much facial or body hair. I don't have to shave every day and when I do it's just over my upper lip, so I can never grow a beard. People often remark on the smoothness of my skin, sometimes insinuating I must wear make-up. I never wear it, even when I'm feeling outrageous. I can't bear tattoos or cosmetic surgery, Botox, liposuction, face-lifts, and all that. Rosa always said celebrities look much worse after having a facelift, with their expressionless eyes and tight smiles. There is no growing old gracefully any more. Rosa did look young for her age and when she dressed up for special occasions she could look stunning in her elegant cocktail dresses or fitted suits and pearls, walking with head held high like a mannequin. She had an eye for colours and I have inherited this.

Other times she looked awful in her old black Astrakhan coat. She hated the wintry cold and wrapped a tartan woollen scarf around her middle, held together with safety pins. I remember when I was nine or ten feeling embarrassed about this, ashamed even. I didn't want anyone discovering that scarf. We always had hot water bottles, up until May.

'Ne'er cast a clout till May be out,' she'd say. I was never sure whether it meant the May blossom or the month of May.

My hot water bottle was an earthenware stone receptacle shaped like a fat submarine with a hole and stopper in the middle of it. Rosa wrapped it in a sock to stop it burning my feet but I still suffered from chilblains. When it was cold and empty I played games with it, imagining it as a German submarine that I blew up. In my other war games I was Brutus, the Polish double agent, helping the British to double-cross the Germans, or I was a British officer constructing dummy aircraft or landing craft in fake embarkation points before the Normandy landings on D-Day.

We weren't poor and we lived quite comfortably although Rosa continually complained about bills. We must have been one of the few households in Dorset Street to have central heating. When I was nine or ten, the Polish priests had it installed mainly for their school but inserted the radiators throughout the entire house. Rosa wasn't accustomed to it and was petrified of spending too much money on gas.

'Now it's April, I'm turning the heating off.'

'What's Hazel got to do with the heating?'

'I said April!'

Rosa was the daughter of Alba and Francesco. Her identical twin brothers, Franco and Vincent, were two years younger. Uncle Franco and Uncle Vince lived in Potters Bar and Rosa said it was too difficult for us to get there and then Franco moved to Barnet, which was even further away. Franco was the uncle I liked most, the one who seemed genuinely fond of me, and he bought me presents. He was more affectionate and outgoing than his brother. Vince was the less forceful one, the quieter of the two. As it was so difficult to tell them apart physically – they even spoke in the same way – with London-Italian accents.

I identified them by their personalities. Rosa didn't have the same accent; she sounded posher, more English.

I don't remember going to Barnet often, once for a cousin's confirmation when I was quite little and a wedding anniversary party in my early teens. It was after that my uncles came to Dorset Street once a month for dinner – on a Monday evening – when their restaurants were closed. The uncles loved slumming it in Dorset Street. We sat round the yellow Formica kitchen table. Rosa instructed me to lay it carefully with her freshly laundered white damask tablecloth, tall fluted wine glasses and old silver cutlery. She always rustled up something tasty – she even cooked veal which she bought from the Italian butcher in Soho.

'You're not eating that, the poor calves are force-fed antibiotics!' I shouted.

She served it with spaghetti in tomato sauce so I was given a double helping.

'Your mum spoils you, Dorek,' said Uncle Vince. Rosa always gave him a hard stare when he said that. I don't think he ever realised I was a veggie.

Sometimes she did roast beef and Yorkshire pudding for her brothers as a treat which they very much appreciated.

'We never get the chance to eat a proper lunch on Sundays as the Mayfair restaurant is always open.'

For me she made a separate Yorkshire cooked in olive oil and I also got extra vegetables. Then for afters it was always apple pie or lemon meringue.

I enjoyed these occasions as they always treated me:

'Here's ten bob for you, Dorek,' said Uncle Vince with a flourish but Uncle Franco always slipped a one pound note into my shirt pocket. When I started wearing hearing aids, he always gave me a five-pound note.

Franco's mother, Angela, my paternal great-grandmother, came from Calabria in the south of Italy. According to Uncle Vince, her father had mafia connections. He was a bookkeeper cum fencing instructor, supposedly, who mysteriously fled to England with his family. Angela had married my great-grandfather, also called Francesco or Franco, and together they had opened a restaurant in Holborn. This had been so successful that my uncles now ran a chain of restaurants called

The Crispin Bars. Funny that the restaurant chain might have been originally funded by mafia money when my uncles tried so hard to be respectable, involved in charitable and cultural pursuits.

Alba, my grandmother, as well as helping with the restaurant business, assisted sick Italians and recently arrived Italian immigrants – or something like that – and my uncles set up a charitable foundation in her honour. Rosa said she and her brothers had a row over money or maybe it was about this foundation, I can't really remember. I know they didn't speak to each other for a while and she was definitely estranged from them when she had me. I never knew the full story until recently. (It's difficult to tell a story chronologically with hindsight, but this is what I have decided to do.) Throughout my childhood and adolescence Rosa made me feel proud of my Italian-Polish heritage. She told me stories about the Italian side quite often and because I grew up without a father, I did feel closer to my Italian family, and to the history surrounding them. The details about my father's family were much more nebulous.

Although I am called Wiadrowski after my Polish father, Rosa went by the name Rosa Crespi. She said it was because Italian women continue to use their maiden names on official documents after they marry. But when my uncles opened their restaurant chain they anglicised the name to Crispin and my mum started calling herself Rose Crispin. I'm still not sure why, possibly because it sounded more English and she wanted to be associated with what by now were becoming the famous 'Crispin' restaurants. I hated my surname because it was virtually impossible to pronounce, especially by me as I have a soft 'R'. When I suggested I also change my name to Crispin, Rosa wouldn't have it. She insisted I keep the Polish name. Sometimes I think that it was because my name began with a W that I usually sat in the back row in classes at school and that's why I couldn't hear. But no one, not even Rosa, realised this at first.

Looking back, I am very grateful I was brought up in England when I was. I benefited so much from the NHS and my education was decent even though I didn't do very well at school. This was obviously related to my undetected deafness, but I loved reading books, visiting libraries or museums, going to the cinema. And when we finally got a television, I enjoyed all the foreign films with subtitles that were broadcast in the sixties. I can remember Roberto Rossellini's *The Bicycle Thieves* and Vittorio de Sica's *Two Women*. The subtitles helped me.

I never learnt Italian formally but having done French at school and with what Rosa taught me, I have a little knowledge of it. Rosa was a great reader and one wall of our flat was covered in books. We had the Encyclopaedia Britannica, the Oxford Dictionary, poetry by Keats, Shelley, Wordsworth, Tennyson and Byron, books on the Italian Renaissance, Greece and Rome, as well as numerous novels she had picked up here and there. She said that her mother Alba had made her read when she was a child, had told her many stories, and she had never stopped reading since. Alba wanted her to be a doctor and had been upset when Rosa decided nursing was what she really wanted to do.

Although Rosa often talked about Alba, she still remains a vague figure to me. I know she was born in 1900 and married before she completed her studies in Milan. Rosa said Alba had a complicated family background. There was talk of her twin, Fabio, who died very young. Shame they had only found out they were brother and sister not long before he died. One day I planned to visit Torretta, where my great-grandmother had lived, to find out more about this mystery. Alba had travelled back to Italy after her mother (I think her name was Raiza) died of a heart attack at the beginning of the Second World War and it took her a while to get back because Italy was the enemy. Switzerland was neutral but she had to skirt round France, crossing the channel eventually from Belgium. Alba was so relieved to get back to England after being stuck in the remote village of Torretta, she never returned to Italy. The awful thing is that from what I could gather, Raiza my great-grandmother detested the idea of Fascist Italy fighting alongside Nazi Germany and was making plans to join Alba in England. Rosa must have been a teenager when this happened and said to me:

'I thought my mother was never coming back. It scarred me and that's when I left childhood behind. The outbreak of war was terrible. Although we were born in London, we were still classed as the enemy because of our Italian heritage. People used to throw stones through our windows where we lived in Holborn.'

Her family lived in the Italian quarter of Clerkenwell (in the Borough of Holborn) at that time and soon after war broke out Alba moved to Hatfield, Hertfordshire. Rosa was packed off to a convent boarding school in Burgess Hill, Sussex for some months. Fortunately my twin uncles were called up to the British Army so weren't interned like many other Italians. Rosa always said she had plans to join the Resistance in France but she was too young. And by the time I was born in 1949, the Londoners I grew up with had mostly forgotten their hatred of Italians under Mussolini. On reflection, the Poles have had a worse time than the Italians. They fought alongside the British but their heroics are largely forgotten, whereas the Italians battled against the British and although they are made fun of for their lack of heroism, they are treated more fondly. I'm no great admirer of military heroism and always chuckle at the standard jokes about Italian cowardice:

'How many gears has an Italian tank got? Five, four for

reversing and one for going forward just in case the enemy attacks from behind.'

Rosa was a bitter person but it wasn't because of the war. It was because her husband Piotr had died so suddenly and she had been left to bring me up on her own. The rift with her family didn't help. She was usually calm and balanced but every so often, perhaps once a month, she'd scream at me.

'Your reports from school are terrible. You're not stupid, why can't you do better?'

At other times, she would be even more vitriolic:

'I've wasted my time on you, never had a husband, never enjoyed life. I haven't had sex since I had you.' This is not something a boy wishes to hear and it fell on my deaf ears. Unconsciously, I switched off during her ranting.

She did go out with men from time to time. I met one or two. One was a taxi-driver called Freddie but it didn't last long. There was another, Uncle Jack; she saw him for a year or two up until I was about fourteen. He bought me the first Rolling Stones EP. I was ecstatic. But soon after, it ended. I'm not sure why. When I asked, she said they never really had anything in common. He was an accountant, had a good job in the city, wanted her to move in with him.

'No, he wasn't my type. It wouldn't have lasted.' Another time she blamed me:

'How could I move in with a man when I'm stuck with you? I couldn't expect Jack to marry me and my son!'

When she was in an affectionate mood, even when I was taller than she was and too old for sitting on her lap, she'd drag me across the room, sit me down on the sofa, and cradle me.

'Oh, my baby, my baby, I love you so much, don't ever leave me,' and she would cover me in kisses. Once she kissed me on my mouth but then she realised what she'd done, withdrew her lips like an Italian retreat, recoiling and shivering in her embarrassment. I can still feel her lips pressed tightly against mine, the taste of her lipstick, like overripe strawberries.

Occasionally I slept with her. After she'd had a nightmare, she'd knock on my door and call me to get into bed with her, which I did reluctantly. She'd hold me in her arms, but it was me comforting her, not the other way round. If I had a nightmare, I tried to write it down, more interested in why I had dreamt such a thing. I never called out to her for any comfort.

She seldom talked about my father. I had to rely on my fantasies about him unless I pestered her with questions. When she became too suffocating or too intimate, I used to walk to the library or get a bus and kick a ball around in Highbury Fields. Or I would meet up with friends from school if there were any around.

A Polish Father

I've always been a loner,
Why am I different? Not sure but
Not everyone's the same.
There are people like me who
Don't want to conform,
Work regular hours,
Eat three meals a day,
Meat and two veg.
I like words. Words are for
Thinking, that's what I want to do – think,
Think about who I am, why I exist.
Think about the world, its problems,
Why people don't live in harmony.
Why we are programmed that way.
The animal kingdom is more ordered,
Preoccupied with survival, food and drink.
The more leisure we enjoy,
The more life gets complex.
We are more disquieted,
Less comfortable with ourselves,
More aimless, less focused.
We worry, we are concerned.
Our sophistication
Makes us discerning but
Ultimately less satisfied.
The successful few are free
From financial worries
Yet still discontent.
What's the meaning of it all?

'Come on, men, we're going to attack the Nazis, get out of this goddamn forsaken place.' Dashing Captain Wiadrowski was in his full battle dress uniform, steel helmet on head, bren gun at the ready.

'Sir, are you mad? There're only ten of us.'

'Doesn't matter, boy, we have to do this. Here, take these!'

Wiadrowski hands the men steel helmets and bren guns. They have appeared by magic. The men are dazzled but they gun down all their guards in a deafening, explosive noise and escape from the camp. They make it.

My father, Captain Wiadrowski, is a hero...

I have a photo of Piotr Wiadrowski in Polish uniform. He has blond hair and is tall like me, with a shy, almost embarrassed grin on his face. In another photo he has a surprisingly dark-looking moustache.

The details about Rosa and him are confusing. Rosa once told me she met him during the war when he was wounded while she was nursing at a military hospital, maybe in Kent somewhere, or Aldershot. But another time she said they met at a party in London, like on a blind date, arranged by a Polish nurse she worked with. I know she had fond memories of the Polish church as they used to go to the social club there in the basement. I never went there, only to the Polish shop, also in the basement, where Rosa instructed me to buy jars of pickles, tinned fruit and pulses.

Rosa never wanted to talk about my dad but I always persisted. So reluctantly she told me this:

After the Germans invaded Poland in 1939 they requisitioned lots of land, including Piotr's father's family farm. The story goes that they were given ten minutes to leave. They were put on army trucks and Piotr, being the eldest son, was separated from his parents and younger brothers and sisters. The family were taken to a transit camp and he was settled on a farm now run by Germans, part of *Lebensraum* – a territory deemed by the Nazis to be necessary for economic self-sufficiency. Piotr had to sleep in a barn and all he was given to eat was half a loaf of bread a day and a few sips of water. Basically, he became a forced farm-labourer. Piotr couldn't bear the harsh conditions and he tried to escape but was soon recaptured by the Germans. As a punishment he was moved to a labour camp, where he was put in solitary confinement for two weeks.

Rosa recounted the details of this story to me once but repeated this part a couple of times:

'The time your dad spent in solitary confinement was the most traumatic time of his life. He said it was very dark and wet, and all he could hear were the dull sounds of dripping water. The monotonous noise was worse than any torture he might have endured.'

(I remember her saying he was very insistent about being buried somewhere dry because of this dreadful experience. Poor Piotr. He is buried in Finchley cemetery. I hope he feels safe and dry there. I have never visited his grave even though I occasionally visit Rosa's. It must be somewhere nearby in the Catholic part but I don't know where. She never went there.)

Piotr escaped again – successfully this time – and managed to join up with the partisans who left South Poland under cover. They eventually arrived in Rome, fighting alongside the American forces in the Free Army. Piotr drove one of their tanks and then worked on their telephone lines. From Italy he headed to France where he accidentally met up with his uncle Waldek, his mother's brother. Waldek had been part of the French Resistance but was now serving as a Polish soldier.

Apparently Waldek's family had moved to France a long time before the war. My grandmother Barbara, her parents and her much younger brother, Waldek, left Poland when he was a baby in 1922. Barbara was sixteen and stayed behind as she was engaged to marry my grandfather and worked on their farm. Her family emigrated because the French government had advertised for Polish miners, so many Poles took this opportunity of leaving Poland for northern France. This always reminded me of the West Indians coming here in the fifties, when London Transport was advertising vacancies as drivers, conductors and guards.

My great-grandfather had been a tailor by trade and after he had done his obligatory six months in the mines, he opened a tailor's shop. Apparently the Poles used to queue up for hours on end to get a made-to-measure suit, as many had come over in the clothes they stood in and of course there was no 'off the peg' in those days.

Waldek was only seventeen when the war broke out. He was a bit of a rebel by all accounts and joined an underground French Resistance movement helping to sabotage Nazi supply trains. Then when he joined the Polish army he was stationed in England and then eventually Scotland, always involved with communications (Rosa was never sure exactly what). After the war he went to college in south London and did an electrical engineering degree. Then he got a job with Morgan Crucible which involved a lot of travelling and speaking several languages – apart from English, French and Polish, he also spoke Italian, German and Spanish. Waldek married a very young French girl who was part of the French Resistance. She could only have been sixteen. Apparently she had lied about her age. They too moved to London after the war and had two children but I never met them. Rosa said Piotr and

Waldek were firm friends, more like brothers than uncle and nephew, but when dad died Rosa never saw Waldek again. She hinted once that he was filled with remorse about my dad's death but I never knew why. I am convinced that Waldek must have been a spy during the war, and that perhaps he also enlisted my dad. They both worked in telecommunications, intercepting Nazi messages and sending them on to London with the French and the Poles working very closely together. Some of the Polish sections in the Resistance were responsible for transport and delivery of equipment or parachuting men to their destinations. I am guessing that Waldek and Piotr were both in the Sabotage section. Their mission was to destroy telephone lines and power lines, draw up barricades on roads and pull down or move telephone poles. When Waldek transferred to England, he was possibly attached to the special centre for monitoring and decoding at Bletchley Park. So he could have been part of the Polish "Enigma" which played a significant role during the Battle of Britain, the Battle of the Atlantic and the invasion of the continent in 1944. The electronics specialists helped with creating the submarine detection system (HFDF – High Frequency Direction Finding). Polish engineers constructed the reversible tank periscope and an anti-aircraft cannon, and British troops were equipped with tens of thousands of these.

Waldek continued to be a spy after the war ended, as I guessed he would have had problems settling into a mundane life after the exciting one he had led as a soldier. Many Poles, even Waldek, who had lived in France, were supposed to be repatriated to Poland. They weren't very welcome in Britain because of the general state of the economy, the lack of work and food shortages. Waldek could have come to some agreement with MI5 to work against the Russians. On the other hand, Piotr had it easier because he married Rosa, who was British-born, but he could have collaborated with Waldek now and then, when Waldek needed extra help or expertise. Piotr liked all the cloak and dagger stuff too.

Rosa said she fell in love with Piotr before the war ended in 1945. They married quickly at Finsbury Town Hall and she was always very vague about what happened after that. I know he became a telephone engineer for the Post Office. They (or we) were supposed to emigrate to America but he must have died before their application papers were accepted. She said I was a tiny baby when it happened. As she never spoke about him much I learnt not to ask but I still wondered about the mysterious circumstances surrounding his death.

The Polish boys at school and others I knew from the Polish church hated the communists for destroying their country. They were very bitter and ardent Catholics in defiance of communism. They never had a bad word to say about the Brits and were grateful their families had been allowed to stay here, though. I get the impression that some of the wartime generation of Poles felt betrayed by the Brits and weighed down by the burden of what happened to their country. I read recently that their history was falsified by the communists in the subsequent fifty years. I also remember some Polish guy at the church saying their role in the last war had been underplayed, not just the role of military intelligence but other Polish contributions. In 1939, after being attacked by the Germans and then the Soviets from the East, the Poles set up a government-in-exile in Paris. When France collapsed in June 1940, they were forced to retreat to London. They commanded troops and ran military intelligence, with agents operating all over Europe. The information was fed directly to MI6, and the London Poles, long before my dad and Waldek arrived here, passed on intelligence to MI6 throughout the war.

I read about the Katyn massacres, ordered by Stalin in 1940 when around 22,000 Poles were murdered by the Soviet secret police in a forest in Russia. One old Polish chap I know here told me the documentation about Katyn was suppressed by Churchill. The Germans were blamed for it rather than the Soviets and apparently the archive of the Home Army, the wartime non-communist Polish underground, has mysteriously vanished. Polish troops helping the Allied cause were involved in capturing Monte Cassino in Italy, losing an appalling number of men.

'The turning point of the war,' he said, 'was when our Polish fighter pilots were victorious in the Battle of Britain.'

Yet their achievements, both military and in intelligence, have stayed unsung and there are no existing MI6 archives about the Polish contribution. He, being part of the older generation of Poles I knew here in London, felt very bitter about this. More recently he told me that after the collapse of communism in 1999, the Anglo-Polish Historical Committee was formed to examine all available records of World War II Polish intelligence operations.

'So finally there has been a long-overdue recognition of the Polish contribution.'

I have this gut feeling that Waldek and Piotr were heavily involved in this intelligence activity, but it has proved difficult for me to research.

I fantasised a lot about how Piotr died. He was a spy, even a double agent for the Brits and because of some transgression had to be killed. Like Alexander Litvinenko, he could have had polonium-201 slipped into his tea by a Russian counterspy. It caused him to die a painful death from radiation poisoning. Or he was killed by a ricin-filled pellet in an umbrella stick like that Bulgarian, Georgi Ivanov Markov.

The Poles of my generation are pretty much integrated and have done well for themselves. All the Polish boys I went to school with have prospered as either businessmen or academics, not surprising really, as their parents used to bribe them to do well in exams. On the other hand the new wave of Polish workers hasn't found it so easy in this anti-European immigration atmosphere yet they only do the menial jobs we lazy Brits (yes I count myself a Brit) refuse to do. It's bloody obvious that this role always falls to migrants as the existing population gets more affluent and educated. And if the affable Nigel gets his way, I dread to think what will happen if we leave Europe.

Meeting Ambrose

Is being deaf like death?
Or just a Freudian slip?
I wrote death
Instead of deaf
On a note.
Am I dead,
Being deaf?
Perhaps.
I am silent
At home,
At my desk
Or in bed alone
Watching, reading
Writing, sleeping
Eating, not talking.
Solitary,
Contemplating
Life.
Not going out much,
A hermit?
Yet travelling
Is my dream.
To Italia, Polska
And other parts of the world
Here I come.
So not yet
Dead.

Surprisingly, I passed the eleven plus because of cheating Sister Primrose and all those exam papers she made us do.

Where I lived in London there was one secondary modern school, Angel Green, which had a terrible reputation. It was very rough and hardly anyone left with any qualifications. Rosa said I was lucky going to a Catholic school as the education I received was much better than that at Angel Green.

I'm getting on my soapbox again but it's my way of letting off some steam. These days I think the problem with education is that schools are encouraged to be competitive. Parents are invited to choose the schools at the top of the leagues. Yet not everyone can attend a good school. 'Failing schools' get less funding and less encouragement and finally they are closed down. Until all schools are treated equally and each local school is encouraged, then faith schools are a secondary issue. Enough of my pamphleteering now…

Somehow I was put into the top stream at St Sebastian's Catholic Grammar School (Rosa's second choice, her first choice being The Jesuit College in Hammersmith) which was between Highgate and Parliament Hill. It closed down a long time ago. It was opposite the girls' French convent boarding school which Clarrie attended. I used to see her in her green uniform leaving her house around the same time as me but she never acknowledged me, not once. I got the 214 bus on City Road but she always caught the train to Gospel Oak from Highbury and Islington, walking or getting the bus there from Upper Street. Even in uniform she looked pretty and as graceful as a dancer. She wore a green blazer, tartan kilt with safety pin and long cuffed beige socks, trimmed in green with a little green hanging flap or tassel. As she walked the other way up our street towards Upper Street, I used to glance back at her, listening to her sturdy brown lace-up shoes faintly tapping on the pavement. I imagined running round the block to meet her, bumping into her accidentally on purpose and starting a conversation, but what would I say? She'd ignore me; pretend she couldn't hear me, so I gave up.

St Sebastian's seemed huge after St Raphael's, with over 300 boys. We sat in alphabetical order so I was in the back row. This was the first time I realised there might be something wrong with my ears but never put two and two together. Sitting at the back of the class, I couldn't hear what the teachers were saying. I thought this was because I was sitting so far away, not like in St Raphael's where the teacher was always so close.

Most of the time I was in a daydream. 'Dee for Dreamer' some boys called me. By this time I was quite tall and still blond. I wore black horn-rimmed glasses which disguised my pale-blue eyes and my squint. As Rosa was dark she always said how pleased she was she'd had a blond, blue-eyed child. I have a niggling suspicion that when she washed my hair with my head bent over the bathroom washbasin, she applied peroxide to my hair secretly with a toothbrush. She always denied it. I opened the bathroom cupboard one day and found the evidence in a jam jar, reeking of bleach. I recognised this same smell that filled my nostrils when she washed my hair.

Another shock: I made it into the football third eleven at school. Possibly because Brother Michael, one of the sports teachers, liked me – too much! He tried to get me to sit on his knee once but I refused and that seemed to encourage him even more. He was always patting me on the head or arm. I played cricket badly in the summer. I was always twelfth man but I enjoyed it until I got a cricket ball in my eye in the lower sixth. My hand to eye coordination wasn't great but I did well enough at football and I enjoyed the tennis lessons.

Mungo (or Gerard as he was called then) always made me laugh with his antics, pretending to be Rod Laver and hitting aces. He became my best friend. In the third year my appetite had increased enormously and at night I used to get out of bed and secretly devour whole packets of ginger, garibaldi, or custard creams biscuits. Mungo came to my house every other Saturday. We played cards, Monopoly or Risk, then watched the football results on TV. Afterwards Rosa presented us a feast of lemonade, cucumber and tomato sandwiches, chocolate-covered marshmallows wrapped in silver and red foil or marshmallows covered in grated coconut on chocolate biscuit bases. At Mungo's house in Holloway where I used to go on alternate Saturdays, his mum, white-haired, plump, pink-faced and always jolly, fed us on Tizer, bacon sandwiches, sausage rolls, wagon wheels, jamboree bags of sweets, sherbet dips and liquorice allsorts. And my favourite, Battenburg cake, pink and yellow coloured sponge squares covered in jam and yellow marzipan. Mungo loved dolly mixtures. I teased him about them mercilessly, 'Eating those girlie sweets again, dolly?'

At school, my favourite subjects were art, English and maths. I also studied Latin for a while. *Amo, amas, amat. Mensa, mensae, mensam* and all that. I loved the words, *pulcher* and *puer* in Latin, beautiful boy... me, I thought.

All the friends I made at school stayed lifelong friends. Strange, but nice... As well as Mungo there was Dino, Walter Danesi, Damien and me. I was called Dee for short. Dino was Italian and an ace football-player, unlike Mungo and me. He could have had a trial with Arsenal if he wanted but he ended up working in the family business, as did Walter. Walter's family were super rich and I wasn't sure why he didn't go to a posher school. Something about him having to learn his own way and not being too over-privileged, I think. They owned wood and brick factories in Italy and ran several businesses in London as well. Every year he used to leave before the school holiday started in the summer term to travel back to Northern Italy with his family. I was always very envious. Later I discovered his family lived in Tortello, where my grandmother Alba was born.

Walter frequently said to me:

'Your name should be Walter, not mine. You're a real Walter Mitty…' He pronounced it 'Valter', as in Italian.

To get my own back, I called him 'Water'.

'Water, what are you talking about? Who is this Valter Meet-tee?'

'Why do you daydream all the time or pretend to be Paul Temple, then?'

Paul Temple was on the radio. He was my favourite detective.

'Cos I want to be a police detective when I grow up, Water.'

Mungo's mother was Italian like mine and his father was Russian. Damien was the outsider in our gang. He was English, very tall with dark hair and wore Clark Kent glasses. I'm not even sure he was a cradle Catholic like most of us at the school who came from Irish, Italian or Polish backgrounds. His parents must have been converts, the worst and most devout of all. Damien was extremely clever and had strange ideas even then. He read a little Nietzsche and declared he was a Nihilist. The one Nietzsche quote I can remember and agree with is:

The individual has always had to struggle to keep from being overwhelmed by the tribe. If you try it, you will be lonely often, and sometimes frightened. But no price is too high to pay for the privilege of owning yourself.

'What's it all for?' Damien would ask. 'There's no god,

no point to life. Why do we care so much about everything? We worry too much, about our health, love, money. Animals just get on with living. Tthey eat, fuck, sleep. They survive.'

He studied Civil Engineering at Imperial College and when he was in his late twenties he had a vasectomy as he never wanted children. I thought this very drastic. Then, lo and behold, when he was fifty, he got married to the ghastly Susannah who was about thirty. Mungo and I were both horrified that he was finally getting hitched. I think, secretly, Susannah did want children but she never told him this. They obviously loved each other, but we still christened them the 'odd couple'.

Mungo: 'I don't believe it. I never thought he'd be doing this.'

Me: 'During this what?'

Mungo: 'You know he's set the date?'

Me: 'He's sent what, where?'

Mungo: 'I meant Damien has set the date for their wedding…'

Me: 'Yeah, I know. They're going to Combodia for their honeymoon.'

Mungo: 'You mean Cambodia!'

Their wedding was a great laugh, held in Leeds Castle in Kent. Damien and Walter who was best man, wore emerald green and scarlet kilts, and Dino, Mungo and me, the ushers, did too… and no, we didn't moon, or whatever it's called.

The rest of us stayed single except for Dino who married an Italian girl, keeping it in the family and all that. Even though I felt more on the edge of society than Damien, and he got married, he was the most nonconformist of my friends in some respects and it was through him I got interested in art and going to galleries.

He took me to see the Terry Frost show at the Serpentine Gallery once. I remember the vibrant, energetic colours. We walked across Hyde Park to reach the gallery passing all those people on their soapboxes. I remember thinking I could never do this. My lack of courage to spout forth in public in this way is overwhelming. Hence my book is my soapbox.

I started to appreciate modern art, video, installations, even performance art. He liked to talk about current shows and events and I liked listening to him, when I could hear what he was saying. Usually we visited galleries together and I didn't need any words. I just looked at what was on offer and digested it. There was one thing involving sound I loved. It was by a woman called Jenny Swansea. We had to walk around a huge room and pick up various headphones positioned in various parts of the space. When you listened to each headphone the sounds emitted were each of the different instruments playing a Vivaldi concerto. It was great and because I could hear the sounds through the headphones so well, I really appreciated the music.

There was one boy at school I hated and he hated me. His name was Nigel Farrell – NF. Now who does that remind me of? Or *National Front* as we nicknamed him. NF was an ugly sod. He picked on me, saying 'Ooooh, Brother Michael's favourite, aren't you?'

'That's cos I'm prettier than you, you elephant.'

That's when he kicked me on the shin in the playground, making me fall. When I got up I grabbed hold of his hand and bent his fingers back as far as I could. He went down like a deflated zeppelin and I never had much trouble with him after that. We just kept out of each other's way. It made me realise that we can't like everyone and we are all 'programmed' differently. Me, for example, I was more interested in saving whales and elephants than eliminating child poverty. The world would be extremely tedious if we all felt the same but that doesn't mean we shouldn't continue to strive for equality.

A story idea I had recently is based on Damien as the *Ambrose* character. Damien did look down on me; thought I had wasted my life, sneered at the infatuation I had with *her*. He wasn't totally amoral but he would approve of this.

Meeting Ambrose

Rob is a regular, nondescript, neither ugly nor overwhelmingly attractive guy, leading an average, quiet life. He has recently moved to London from Newcastle and is working for a computer software company on Euston Road. He is lonely and hasn't made many friends yet. He's in his early twenties, rather naïve and has never had an intimate relationship with either sex, but thinks he is slightly more attracted to men than to women. He starts using social media and gay websites. He finds a very attractive male on the *Put It There* website. His name is Ambrose. He is tall, dark and languid *(bearing a remarkable resemblance to Damien)*. They are mutually attracted and start a flirtatious correspondence. They soon arrange to meet at the National Gallery in front of Antonio and Piero del Pollaiuolo's *The Martyrdom of Saint Sebastian*. It takes Rob a while to find the right room but he is early and has time to study the painting, an odd construction at first glance, almost like a pyramid of acrobats in awkward poses. He can't decide if he finds it erotic or not; some of the men look more appealing than others. He is intrigued and puzzled by the subdued colours and the various background details such as the men on horseback. He feels relieved and happy when Ambrose finally arrives, looking flamboyant in blue blazer, crisp white shirt, blue- and white-dotted cravat and corn-yellow slacks. Ambrose kisses him on both cheeks, which makes Rob blush a deep crimson. They have coffee in the rather lovely, quaint fifties' top floor café and Ambrose says:

'Do you like the ballet?'

Rob has never been to a ballet but he nods his head.

'I have tickets for *Sleeping Beauty* this Friday at Covent Garden. I would be delighted if you came with me.'

After the ballet, which Rob finds captivating, they have dinner together at Ambrose's London flat in Camden, but no sex. Ambrose doesn't touch Rob once and Rob realises he's relieved about this. Then the next weekend Ambrose says he wants Rob to meet his aunt Ida at Hangar's End in Surrey.

'Do come down to Hangar's End and meet the Aunt. I am sure Ida will be delighted to meet you.'

Ambrose says the house is actually his but he lets Ida live there.

'Poor darling, she's my only surviving relative and I'm her sole heir.'

Ambrose had mumbled something about his parents dying in a car accident but Rob couldn't hear him very well and doesn't like to ask him to repeat the story.

Ida, who looks like a prim Victorian matriarch, is very frail but quite animated at times. She's very excited at meeting Rob and says:

'I have so few visitors. Do come and visit me again any time you wish. I love company!'

Soon Ambrose has persuaded Rob to travel down to Surrey three times a week after work to help with her care, saying:

'You can stay overnight whenever you please, especially if I'm busy in London or wherever.' Rob has no idea if Ambrose means he's occupied with work or whether he will be entertaining a lover.

Aunt Ida is very happy with the arrangement. She too is lonely and she and Rob have hit it off. Rob looks forward to going there after work. He often stays the night and doesn't mind the short commute to work in the mornings. He never has much else on and finds he's now no longer so interested in pursuing his relationship with Ambrose. He is still mystified about what Ambrose does for a living and about him as a person. He seems to enjoy a high standard of living without having any proper job – all very mysterious. Ambrose calls what he does 'wheeling and dealing'. Rob now finds his pomposity rather overbearing and prefers having more down to earth conversations with Aunt Ida. One of the first times Rob went down to Hangar's End, Ambrose showed him how to administer the high dosage of pills and medicines his aunt has been prescribed to take.

'As she's so forgetful, it's better that you give them to her when you're here or at least set them out for her on her plastic tray. It's divided into days, see here, and set up a glass of water with it, if you're not staying.' He made Rob feel like a hired nurse.

In one of their conversations, when Rob is administering her pills and giving her spoonsful of her tonic, Aunt Ida starts describing her idyllic childhood.

'I was born here, you know, and I will die here. I have always loved this beautiful house. It's mine, you know, not Ambrose's, even though I have an inkling that he tells people it's his. That certainly isn't true. After my poor sister died along with her young husband, my parents left it entirely to me. Their car blew up, you know, no one knows for sure why. Ambrose was packed off to boarding school and spent the occasional holiday here but mostly went to his father's family in Dorset.'

One evening Ambrose travels to see his aunt on one of the days that he knows Rob won't be there. He takes his aunt's hands in his and says:

'Darling Aunt Ida, seeing that you have become so fond

of Rob, can I persuade you to change your will? I feel guilty that you're leaving everything to me. Why not include something for Rob?'

She agrees instantly. She didn't need much persuading.

'Why of course, what a good idea!'

She phones her solicitor the next morning and bequeaths a substantial amount to Rob while still leaving the house and the rest of her estate to Ambrose. Two days later, the old dear is found dead in bed by her cleaning lady, Agnes Duckworth. From an overdose of barbiturates, it seems. In her panic and confusion, Agnes calls the police, then an ambulance, and even the fire brigade. Fortunately Ambrose arrives unexpectedly while the ambulance is there and before his aunt's body is taken away for an autopsy.

'I just happened to be passing this way,' he says, 'and saw all this mighty commotion.'

Ambrose tries to calm down the by-now hysterical Agnes.

'All those sleeping pills she swallowed...'

'Now, Mrs Duckworth, do calm down and sit down here in the drawing room. Let me make you a nice cup of hot tea and I'll sort everything out from now on. I can hear the doorbell. I'll go and answer. You stay here now. It must be the police already. I'll show them into the library rather than allowing them to disturb you here.'

'Ah, Chief Inspector and ah, Sergeant, do come in. I think I have an idea of what may have happened to my poor aunt here...'

After a speedy police investigation, Rob is interrogated, as his fingerprints are discovered all over the pill containers and medicine bottles. A bewildered Rob is promptly arrested for Aunt Ida's murder and Ambrose visits him in remand prison.

'Dear old chap, what can I say? I promise I'll do all I can

to help you. So sorry I never answered all your calls before now. It's been such a shock and so much to do, but I'm here now, you sweet thing.'

Ambrose strokes Rob's knee under the table in the room where visitors are allowed to see prisoners.

'I'll find you the best brief I can.'

Unfortunately the solicitor and barrister Ambrose hires don't have much of a case to put up for his defence and Rob is found guilty. He is sent to prison for a life-term. What he ascertains during the trial is that the crucial evidence appears to be that Rob knew he was a beneficiary in her will and killed her for her money. Rob has continued to deny this several times but Ambrose in court says that he was present when his Aunt Ida told Rob she was leaving him a considerable amount of money in return for his friendship and kindness in caring for her.

Ambrose had previously said in the witness box, 'I must admit I thought it was odd that Rob spent so much time with my aunt. But I really thought that they were genuinely fond of each other.'

When he is called to the witness box by his defence, Rob is in tears:

'I had no idea whatsoever Aunt Ida was leaving me anything!'

After he is dispatched to his prison cell to serve his life sentence, Rob never receives another visit from Ambrose. In fact he never hears any more from him. The only news he gets of him is from an old antiques dealer friend who writes to Rob, saying that 'Ambrose has embarked on a world cruise, having inherited his aunt's entire estate, the wily old beggar, with no more word to any of his friends.'

Rob knows that as a prisoner on a life sentence he can't benefit from an inheritance. And so it slowly dawns on Rob that Ambrose has arranged the entire charade.

'The bastard, he planned the whole thing... he set me up... he went prowling for stupid people like me who use those pathetic websites.

'Ambrose was never attracted to me. He knew I was a sucker for flattery. That I could be easily led, both as a sexual and social innocent. He used me, killed his own aunt, framed me then ran off with all her money.'

Rob held his head in his hands. Somehow he would prove his innocence, or if not, find a way to slash his wrists. He couldn't bear to be locked up with all those criminals, degenerates, druggies, poofs and paedos.

I showed Damien my story: 'Not bad,' he said quietly, which for him was high praise. He then changed the subject:

'So, what about these paedophiles coming out of the woodwork and finally being prosecuted? All formerly venerated by the media. The bloody BBC are the worst culprits, covering it all up. They were tolerated, even protected, but why?'

'Yeah, they're all second-rate, mostly talentless. Jimmy Savile was a creep, we all knew that. Rosa used to switch off the television whenever she saw him.'

'Seeing him and Maggie sucking up to each other was sickening. And that Rolf Harris couldn't paint. That picture he did of the Queen is absolutely awful.'

'Men like them are protected by similar, unprincipled men preying on the weak and vulnerable. All very easy for them to cover it all up.'

'No one's courageous enough to say enough is enough. And the pop stars are just as bad. Have you heard the gossip about "Puppy"?'

'Poppy?'

'There's lot of stuff going on. There's an enquiry about

what they all got up to in the eighties. There's even talk that Jill Dando was murdered on instructions from an establishment figure as she was just about to reveal a high-ranking paedophile ring.'

'Yeah, but they have these enquiries which take endless time and expense, then they all get exonerated in the end. Think of Leveson. The newspapers continue to print lies. And the powerful continue to get away with everything, even murder.'

(I always liked Jill Dando, straightforward, no-nonsense, attractive, an outdoor type of girl... I thought it odd she got murdered the way she did. And weird that they imprisoned the wrong person.)

A Funny Old Life

I want to believe,
Seeing and hearing
Kings College Cambridge choir
On Christmas Eve,
Divine descants,
Absolutely perfect acoustics
In the fanned ceiling chapel.
The baby Jesus doll lying in a manger,
Symbol of poverty, abstinence and humility.
In our contrariness we have idolised
The opposite.
Our gods are riches, greed and pride
Gods have not served us well.
Christ's teachings are unheard.
Human suffering is unseen
In the obsession with market forces.
Banks, profits for the few;
Bonuses, out of all proportion
To the contribution they have made
To the common good.
While the rest of us languish
In despair...

I am not a spiritual person. I believe in the here (not hear) and now. Yet for most of us spirituality is very important. Writing, especially poetry, is like prayer. That's what one of my favourite poets, Derek Walcott, has written. He never separates the writing of poetry from prayer. He grew up believing it is a vocation, a religious vocation. The experience of being a poet feels that the body is melting into what it has seen. The 'I' is not important. He says *"That is the ecstasy[...]. It's a benediction, a transference. It's gratitude, really. The more of that a poet keeps, the more genuine his nature."*

Prayers, Mass or Benediction don't do much for me. Being educated at Catholic schools, having all that religion force-fed down my throat made me realise that religion is man-made; gods are created by us to help us cope with pain and suffering, or even to let us off the hook.

When I was at St Raphael's, Benediction was held every Wednesday afternoon when we all trooped into St James church next door. We saw it as an opportunity to play games. At that time the church had a gallery below the bell tower. We used to climb up there, ostensibly to watch the spectacle: the priests in their embroidered white and gold robes, the monstrance, the solemnity. The excessive use of incense did, one could say, evoke mystery, even magic, but we were more interested in playing cards. It was an excuse for us to have some forbidden fun. I did love the Benediction hymns, though and when I heard the singing of *Tantum Ergo* in Andy Warhol's *Lonesome Cowboys*, my favourite film of his, it was a real hoot and such a delightful surprise.

I attempt to write about my life but I am constantly distracted by other things. My opinion on politics or religion, that kind of thing. Or I want to note down my story ideas. It's hard to write about my mother so I have been putting it off...

Rosa and I enjoyed a relatively calm existence. We argued of course and I can't say I was particularly happy but she looked after me. We bumbled along.

It amazes me when writers can remember complete conversations verbatim from when they were young. I remember very few. When I went to those creative writing classes, I was informed dialogue was of the utmost importance. You had to get it right. Being deaf, I find dialogue hard to write. And Rosa and I didn't really have any meaningful conversations about life, politics, or philosophy. I kept my personal opinions to myself. When I look back, we didn't converse a great deal and that's why she never realised I had a hearing problem until quite late.

She was very meticulous, kept the flat immaculately tidy, was fastidious in everything and I suppose instilled the same obsessions in me. I can't say I took that much notice of what she said although it could have been my deafness.

When she was making sure I was ready for school in the morning, one of our conversations could have been something like this:

Rosa: 'The bottom of your shirt is sticking out of your blazer, tuck it in.'

Me: 'Eh? I haven't got a bottle in my shirt.'

Sometimes I did it purposely, making silly puns based on word confusion:

'Do you fancy spaghetti with veal mince tonight?'

'What, Vince meal, what's that? Is he having a dinner party?'

When I answered stupidly like this, she used to stop talking to me, rather than repeat herself.

I share her love of clothes and continued wearing the blues she dressed me in as a child. Denim shirts in pale blue, dark blue, medium blue, and jeans of course, or sometimes beige chinos. I often wore a tan velvet waistcoat or dark brown velour bomber jacket.

When I look back and think of *her* dressed up to the nines in her party clothes, although I envied her and wanted to be her, I didn't want to wear her dresses. I prefer men's clothes, shirts and trousers, so much easier than wearing skirts and unmanageable tights. I liked puffer jackets – I had a shiny bottle-green one with white piping around the shoulders. In winter I wore black or navy-blue polo neck sweaters and a navy-blue reefer jacket. I also owned a blazer with brass buttons and although I didn't have the opportunity to wear it often, it looked good with my blond wavy hair and chiselled cheekbones. People often said I looked like Laurence Harvey, the actor. I was secretly pleased although I always refuted the idea that I looked anything like him. I was blond!

Leather was a problem. I couldn't bear the idea of animals being slaughtered for their hides to make footwear. And as for fur, just don't get me onto that subject.

When I was sixteen, about the same time I started wearing hearing aids, I decided I couldn't wear leather any more. So I bought canvas shoes in summer, Gortex walking boots (making sure there was no leather in them) or wellies in winter, sometimes even galoshes. And I always wore long sleeves, even in summer, as I hated exposing my bare hairless arms. I got into the habit of wearing a navy-blue padded jerkin with multi pockets although when the weather was bad, I was particularly fond of my beige gumshoe raincoat. I fancied being a spy or a private detective… and men's clothes are so much more practical.

I have never experimented with cross-dressing. I hate them trannie clothes, especially those frilly things some of them wear. I once saw a bloke pedalling a bike; he had stubble all over his chin and was wearing a mustard-coloured transparent lacy blouse, a tight purple skirt riding up his thick hairy thighs, and high-heeled white court shoes squeezed onto his big, bony, bunioned feet. I feel sympathy for the transgender/gender-confused person and anyone in that situation should receive as much psychological and financial help as possible. On the other hand, I have never wanted to be a woman physically. I would never want to have female breasts or have my dick chopped off for that matter. I do feel sorry for the chaps who've had hormone treatment for prostate cancer with their pendulous breasts.

Rosa always bought me special little treats: Floris dark chocolates, fine lawn white handkerchiefs, Pringle tartan socks; once a light-brown cashmere V-necked sweater.

'My lovely boy deserves it,' she said, stroking my lean smooth cheeks with both her hands. Funny that I could always hear her compliments rather well but not her nagging.

And then everything changed. When she died, a passer-by who comforted me said:

'She just kindled over at the bus stop.' I didn't know what she meant and then I realised:

'She just keeled over at the bus stop.'

She must have thought I was really gormless because I just stared at her. I remember saying:

'Sorry, sorry, sorry…' and that's all. I didn't cry though.

It was early evening in June. We were running for the number 19 bus at the Angel, going to Shaftesbury Avenue. We were going to see *Butch Cassidy and the Sundance Kid,* which had just come out.

When I finally saw it I will never forget that part when they are stuck on a high cliff with a long drop into cascading water:

'You only jump if you have to.'

'I can't swim.'

'Well, the fall will kill you anyway.'

After Rosa's death I felt I had to make that jump, even if it killed me anyway.

Rosa obviously had a weak heart – a hereditary defect. High cholesterol was what it said on the death certificate although she never had it tested. It wasn't that common in those days to have the blood test, and being a nurse, she thought she was above illness, heart conditions, whatever, and shrugged things off. I don't ever recollect her being sick enough to take a day off work. Not yet 50, so younger than her mother Alba when she died.

When she fell over, she coiled up like a baby still in the womb. I was in a daze, paralysed, my knees trembling. Someone called an ambulance, which arrived instantly, and the paramedics put her face-up on a stretcher. We went together to Bart's – St Bartholomew's Hospital – in Smithfield. She was pronounced dead on arrival. A nurse must have asked me for some family contacts. At first I couldn't remember any telephone numbers, except the one in the hall at Dorset Street – *Canonbury 2244*. Then Uncle Franco's telephone number miraculously came into my head. Well, the number of the Crispin Bar in Mayfair – *Whitehall 2121* – did. Next thing I remember, he and Uncle Vince were taking care of everything. All the arrangements didn't take much longer than ten days. Coroner, death certificate, undertaker in Theobald's Road, the funeral at the Italian church and afterwards a reception at their flagship Mayfair restaurant. The food at the wake was delicious: spinach flans, a tasty potato pie, tomato salads, green salads, celery, fennel, pickled artichokes, grilled red peppers, olives and flat bread, lots of red wine. I remember stuffing myself full and drinking glass after glass of Chianti from those fat bottles covered in straw.

My mum was dead. I was nearly nineteen. I got very

drunk and very sick. I was shocked and upset but I didn't cry and the world was my oyster, or so it seemed.

After the funeral I insisted on going back to the flat in Dorset Street. Uncle Franco put me in a taxi and stuffed wads of notes in my blazer pocket.

Later, I have this recollection of going to see a film at the Curzon. It was about a gay man, a very daring, avant-garde topic in those days and about the aversion therapy he underwent. Looking at male nudes, he was forced to vomit. Seeing this film and my confusion about my sexuality, or rather lack of it, has stuck in my mind.

Scene shifting back to the present, I know now that I'm asexual. In my heart of hearts, I knew I wasn't gay. I preferred women, their softness, their silkiness. My fantasy woman would be small-breasted with long dark curly hair – like her. Yet I can't imagine having sex with anyone, let alone anal sex or giving a blowjob to a man, I could neither be a 'giver' nor a 'taker', as Damien pointedly described gays. He thought he was good at judging guys who either preferred buggering or who preferred to be buggered. I loathe the masculinity of men, muscles, hairy backs, hairy shoulders, even beards. But then again, I couldn't imagine having sex with a woman either. I have dreamt about penetrating a woman, but am never able to perform. I believe I suffer from a condition called 'erectile dysfunction'. I loved the idea or 'romance' of being in love with a woman but not its physical manifestation. Rosa must have guessed this. She knew I'd never had a relationship and apart from my obsession with Clarrie across the road, I have never wanted one.

I read this recently and want to make a note of it:

Testicles for tea

In 2012, Japanese artist Mao Sugiyama had his genitals surgically removed, to raise awareness of asexual rights. After keeping them in the fridge for a while, he cooked them and served his friends a meal of steaming hot bollocks. But was it art? Hard to say without actually tasting them.

Manolo Blahnik, he of the famous shoes, about himself:

I don't fall in love with people, I fall in love with art. Relationships for me are a no-no. Imagine having to talk to someone all the time or waking up with them breathing all over you. Not for me at all. I find it very uncivilised. Life lessons aren't really important. Remain dignified, dress well, be good to other people and you'll be fine.

The Curzon film made me feel uncomfortable. I had never really thought about whether I was gay. I wasn't aware of fancying other men. I had never had a girlfriend but then again I'd never had a boyfriend. In the film the gay man is a fitness fanatic and frequents a gym with other gay men displaying their pectorals and biceps...

I thought I should also join a gym but I never did. I'd always been teased at school for being weedy. The character in the film says that you develop a false sense of self-image. It's so true. When I look in the mirror, I don't see who I really am. To some extent I am narcissistic. I kissed a similar-looking blond boy once in the St Seb's changing rooms. He was a born-again freak, part of the God Squad and he pushed me away violently, but it was like kissing myself and I wasn't even aroused.

I don't feel I know myself, know who I really am. In

the film, the character became very destructive and turned to steroid abuse, sunbeds, and, horror of horrors, cosmetic surgery…

And that set me thinking about Scientology. Two of my gay acquaintances joined in the seventies. And so did many celebrities like Tom Cruise and John Travolta. They seem to have need of an organisation or a leader telling them what to do. Saying it's wrong to be gay, saying that men have to get married and have families. All religions, even a contemporary one, prey on the weak and vulnerable, such as people who have problems with their homosexuality. Strong personalities have power over weak people, and money always comes into it as well. The Church of Scientology must be extraordinarily rich by now, yet a religion should not be profit-making. Scientologists don't give to the poor, they take from them. People still need a doctrine, need to be told how to conduct their lives. I don't really understand it. Gods, religion, power. Marx was right: the opium of the people. It's old hat now, but as Damien says, we still crave a reason for living, a crutch, a prop to get through life. And if we are rich and/or uncomfortable with being gay, Scientology seems to offer a solution. I think L Ron Hubbard just got lucky. People read his books, and as he was a very forceful, influential character, it took off from there. It's almost a joke, the fact that he hoodwinked so many people and his Scientology organisation continues to do so.

At Rosa's funeral in Finchley crematorium, the priest ad-libbed about her life. He had quizzed Uncle Franco beforehand, and as funerals go it wasn't too bad, but at no time did I sense anything religious or spiritual. No god was present. Rosa was dead and burnt, and I had to adjust to that, somehow… Her ashes were eventually buried in the family plot there in the cemetery.

Well, one thing was clear to me. I wasn't going to stay on

at St Sebastian's School. I had managed to get four O levels in art, maths, English Language and English Literature. I was retaking geography and history, which I liked, and had started A levels in art, maths and English. Rosa had wanted me to take up biology again, but I hated it. When Mr Malone, the biology teacher, dissected that mouse, it was the final straw. So I gave up doing A levels and resits. I wasn't doing well in any case. I failed maths mock with 27%. We had a new teacher, Mr Didcot. He took us to see a lecture about the *Five Dimensions* which freaked me out. And he mumbled.

The week after Rosa died I had missed my first art exam. I decided that I could always do art and English later. What I really wanted to do was start working.

I stayed with Uncle Franco for a while at his home in Barnet. His two sons were grown up and married, so he and his wife Doreen welcomed me with open arms. They had plenty of room in their mock-Georgian mansion. He got me a job at the *Crispin Bar* in Oxford Circus. I hated it. I buggered up the coffee machine on my first day and never really recovered from it. The rest of the staff ignored me, maybe because I was the boss's nephew, and I ignored them in return, mainly as I couldn't hear in all the noise a bustling, busy restaurant makes. In those days hearing aids didn't eliminate any background noise.

On a whim, I gave up the job and took a typing course at a college in Moorgate. I had always loved the toy typewriter I'd had as a child. It didn't have a keyboard but a dial with all the letters on it. You turned it to the letter you wanted, pressed the dial down and it got stamped onto the paper in the machine. I wrote very short, silly stories on it for hours. Today it would be called micro-fiction.

When I started at the college, I bought myself a new portable Olivetti. The course was for secretaries and I was the only male. The girls were friendly, one was too friendly and was always asking me out. I politely declined each time, making the excuse I had a sick mother to look after. Liar.

I failed the shorthand exam, but I did learn how to touch-type which has stood me in good stead, especially for typing this memoir. There was a small temping agency run by a Miss Petra Finch near the college so I took a series of temping jobs, copy-typing letters, legal documents and accounts sheets, even some bookkeeping. I worked at EMI for a short stint working out musicians' royalties. That's where I learnt how to use an electric typewriter, which was useful. Petra seemed very fond of me and always got me good jobs which paid very well. Some of the men I worked for didn't like the idea of a male secretary. One man on the first morning of a new job yelled at me for typing one word wrong, so I just walked out. I'd had enough of restaurants and offices. I felt claustrophobic working inside.

So then I got a job as a labourer, a hod carrier. But I didn't stick it. It was heavy work and I wasn't into the banter, the macho camaraderie of the others. Wolf-whistling at all the girls, dirty jokes, repetitive boring sexual innuendo. They didn't know what to make of me, and when they finally learnt to leave me alone, I decided to give up the job. After that I left London and went to Norfolk for a while and lived in a caravan. I helped a girl look after sheep; she was a real shepherdess – called Eileen Lamm! Yet I always thought of her as 'Little Bo Peep'. Well, not so little. I remember on one awful evening she made rice pudding from a sheep's first milk after lambing and she even put in the baby lamb's placenta. It was called 'beastlings' or 'bislings' or something like that, and was full of blood and absolutely disgusting. I vowed to become vegan after that experience, but it was more difficult than I thought it would be. I do still drink soy milk and soy yoghurts. I eat pulses, fruit, vegetables and salad. Sometimes rice, couscous, bulgur wheat, quinoa. My mainstay is a salad of chopped tomatoes and grated carrot with a can of borlotti beans.

I cook with olive, sunflower, linseed, rape-seed and soya oil. I lapsed slightly, especially after that trip to Italy. I now eat pasta made with egg, whereas in the past I bought egg-free or made my own. My Eureka moment was discovering Italian ice cream. I do still have soy ice cream, but too often I get tempted by *fior di latte, vaniglia, pistachio,* or *limone,* all made with skimmed cow's milk. Then as a natural progression, I started eating goat's and sheep's cheeses, even buffalo mozzarella. I still don't use Parmesan, but Pecorino, which is sheep's cheese, is great grated, ha ha...

After sheep, I changed to fruit picking, but only lasted four weeks. I had an argument with the apple farmer, Richard Bottomley. He always called me 'Doris' or 'Nancy boy' and made snide remarks about my long hair in his drawling Norfolk accent.

'Had it blow-dried this morning, have ya?'

When I first met him I asked if he was from New Zealand, so we didn't get off to a good start... As you can guess, I am pretty hopeless at accents.

Every day he shouted at me, saying I was slower than the others and wasn't picking the apples fast enough. It was harder than it looked, and sometimes I couldn't manage to keep the little stalk in the apples which meant they couldn't be sold.

'Doris, you're the slowest picker I've ever had. You fairies are useless.'

'You can stick your stupid job up your stupid fat arse, you stupid fat dick.'

Then I tried gardening at a stately home just into Suffolk. I loved watching the plants grow, but gardening didn't love me. All that dirt under my hands finally got to me... Actually I developed a skin allergy to plants in the acacia family and my arms became covered in a rash – like very bad eczema. And my back wasn't holding up very well with all that digging. Some days I could barely walk. I went to the local GP who sent me off immediately for X-rays at Ipchester Hospital (they did that in those days) and I was told I had an over-mobile segment in one of the vertebrae at the base of my spine. Digging was not advised.

When I got back to London I applied for a civil service job at the Ministry of Defence. Unsurprisingly I didn't get an interview. I reckon it was my surname...

I started seeing Mungo, as he came to be known (nicknamed after Mungo Jerry, a rock band briefly famous for their one hit '*In the Summertime*' in 1970), and going to the Italian club in Clerkenwell on top of St Paul's Italian church. His sister Yolanda came with us, and I met up with Dino and Walter Danesi from school and got to know Tony who played the accordion. They often held dinner dances. I liked the dinner part (they always made me special vegetarian food) but I never joined in the dancing. I have two left feet and no sense of rhythm. Needless to say, I have retained my feelings of inadequacy about singing or dancing. Some people I know are multi-talented. As well as being highly intelligent, they are great singers and dancers with a great ear for music – but not me!

Plus I wasn't particularly interested in asking a girl to dance in any case. Mungo was good at dancing but he was too shy to ask any female to be his partner. He was confident about everything else; sounded like a comedian when he talked, but when it came to women he just froze.

The only women I became friendly with were the sisters Luella and Luanna who had anglicised their surname from Gregorio to Gregory. I'm still friendly with them. Back in the

70s, they looked like twins, with their dark hair swept up in French pleats and elaborate butterfly glasses over their brown eyes. They were cousins of Mungo and best friends with Yolanda. They too never married. They had risen high up in the Foreign Office, past the glass ceiling and beyond. I always thought they could be spies for MI5, even double agents. I imagined them carrying out cloak and dagger operations deep in the innards of Whitehall or meeting other spies in smart places such as Fortnum and Mason's, pretending to be enjoying tea and cakes but intent on plotting someone's downfall. Who'd ever suspect two upright ladies? They are still peculiarly left-wing on some issues. They thought British imperialism had a lot to answer for. Well, I agreed with them there. Their view was that the Iron Curtain was a good thing. The Communists suppressed civil wars, religion, poverty, crime, and from a Western point of view, with all this anti-immigration feeling now, maybe they were right. The European market would be much smaller with much less freedom of movement for Eastern Europeans to travel within the Community. They said it should have been limited to the original six members, and with hindsight maybe they are right about that too. The euro might have worked better.

'The EU is too unwieldy and corruption is rife,' they repeatedly argued. 'It's impossible to manage the single currency when each country is so politically diverse and struggling against recession. After the collapse of the Berlin Wall, the Tories were wrong to encourage EU expansion from Eastern Europe.'

I always tried to add my two pennies' worth:

'In my opinion there should be a two-tier Union. The countries inside the euro should be governed like one state, and those outside, while having the same commercial rules, should have fewer legal and financial restraints imposed on them.'

'Yes, Dee, of course, how succinct!'

'What's sex-linked?' I was starting to make up these homonyms just for the fun of it… rather than because of my deafness.

Today, the immediate problem is how UKIP are exploiting the fact that people are worried about EU immigrants flooding into this country. They have raised the alarm and exaggerated the problem, but actually, the numbers are very low, a small percentage of the total UK population.

'In the past, I even prophesied that the Brits wouldn't want Eastern Europeans flooding the country.'

'Well, it's making a mountain out of a molehill,' said Luella, or was it Luanna?

Luella and Luanna were another 'odd couple', or rather I should say 'quartet'. They had two cousins called Laura and Loretta. Their Italian mothers (Mungo's maternal aunts) had married two Irish brothers. They all looked like sisters, even 'quads' or, as we called them, *the four Elles*.

Loretta was the butchest-looking of the Elles (especially now with her cropped white hair and the sheepskin coat she always wears). Laura and Loretta were also civil servants, working at the Home Office. They too could have been spies, working for the Russians, trading Home Office and foreign secrets. The Elles often went on holiday together. For civil servants they had long periods of leave and were always off on jaunts to Moscow, St Petersburg, Burma, Cuba, even China. They always chose countries ruled by dictators or totalitarian regimes. Baffling. They were booked to go to Baghdad just before the Iraqi war started. Their antagonism towards Tony Blair was more to do with the cancellation of their holiday than his suspect reasons for intervention. And they didn't think too badly of Saddam Hussein, the 'lesser' of two evils, they said. They predicted the country would collapse after his overthrow.

I enjoy discussing politics with them. They're the only ones who listen to my views of the world. They tease me mercilessly, but I enjoy it.

'Dee, you're quite opinionated under that quiet exterior. Have you ever thought about going into politics?' asked Luella.

'Well, I'm thinking of it… I have drawn up my manifesto. Shall I tell you about it?'

'Why, of course, we're all ears. Forgive me… Dee… yes, please do,' said Luanna.

I pretended to unroll my scroll, but this was another fantasy. I never told them what I seriously had in mind…

Crispin's Manifesto

Stop vivisection and all other cruelty to animals.
Save all species in danger of extinction.
Tackle climate change.
Change to alternative energies.
Save NHS from privatisation.
Drug companies should be penalised for overpricing.
Renationalise railways and the Post Office.
Renationalise all utilities. Keep them British.
Make all motorways toll roads.
Introduce congestion charges in all major cities.
Introduce building incentives for public housing.
Build more single-person units.
Scrap bedroom tax.
Councils to pool pension funds on national basis.
Stop selling council property.
Churches and other societies to run loan schemes.
Establish state bank.
Stop business cartels and multinational dominance.

Education should be run by an impartial councils.
Abolish entire civil list.
Remain part of Europe.
I could go on...

I still see Luella, Luanna and Loretta from time to time. Laura died quite recently so now they are the three Elles. They play bowls at St James Church where I sometimes still go with Dino and Walter.

Dino continued playing football for Sunday League teams. He still occupies the same house where he was born, next door to where Joe Orton used to live... I saw Joe Orton and the odd-looking Kenneth Halliwell once or twice walking alongside the gardens in Douglas Terrace. Joe looked very young and healthy. It was a shock to read in the newspapers he'd been battered to death by Kenneth It was odd they lived together. Joe was so handsome compared to plain Kenneth. Another 'odd couple'.

There were a couple of queers, as gays were called in those days, who often walked past my door in Dorset Street. I imagined them frequenting the Islington Green cottage but I never dared go there, even when I was desperate for a pee. Later when I read *Prick Up Your Ears* I understood why Joe Orton was not interested in conventional courtship. He wanted rough sex with strangers. That's what turned him on, but I found that totally terrifying.

We were all football fans, supporting our local team, Arsenal. I was really into football from the seventies to the nineties. I loved the atmosphere created by the boisterous, exhilarated crowd with their London-humour-inspired chanting at home games, although Dino quite often had to tell me what they were singing. The best game I ever watched was Arsenal at home to Moscow Dynamo. The Russian players moved across the pitch like dancers and Arsenal emulated them. I have come to love ballet and have seen performances of *Corsaire*, *Nutcracker*, *Sleeping Beauty*, *Swan Lake*, *Firebird* with *Petrushka* a few times now, but that game was the first to remind me that accurate passing football is a joy to watch.

Most seasons we drove to away games at Leeds, Liverpool and Manchester. It was still the time of standing on the terraces. Arsenal scored against Manchester United once at Old Trafford. The noise was incredible and we all surged forward and I ended up doubled over on one of the barriers and bashed my groin badly. I was lucky I didn't do myself a nasty injury... not that I would have missed it that much...

Strangely, when Arsenal became an all-seater stadium I became disillusioned with football. Too much money swirling around for television rights; Sky dictating when games should be played; spoilt whinging players. Even Denis Bergkamp, one of my idols, refused to fly to games. If he didn't play in a match, then he shouldn't be paid. And Georgie Best and Paul Gascoigne both ruined by drink or drugs. Not a great example for the future generations of how to behave.

The insidious racism also got to me: the monkey chants and gestures. Instead of improving race relations with more and more black players on the pitch, it seemed to get worse. And the final straw was the unspoken subject of gay footballers. It was obvious there must be some gay men amongst footballing ranks. There was gossip about who was gay, but no one ever came out until the tragic Justin Fashanu. That's when I stopped going. Then there's *Septic Bladder*, a vile receptacle for receiving and doling out bribes. Apparently FIFA spends more on operating expenses, such as wages and travel, than it does on 'football development', which is only a tiny part of its annual budget. And he refuses to retire!

A gay footballer
When I was three,
I liked dressing up,
Wearing pink feather boas
And high-heeled shoes.
Mum and Dad laughed.
Thought it was a giggle,
But when I got to school
Only girls wore pink.
So I toned it down
And played computer games,
But football was the best.
Became first team centre forward
Kept it quiet that
I liked boys not girls.
At secondary school
I met other boys like me.
I told my parents.
They said 'wait and see.'
When our team went out post-match
They looked at girls
And turned a blind eye
At me watching boys.
They only cared about my goals.
Volleying the ball into the net,
Or making a diving header
To score a match-winner –
The best feeling in the world.
To celebrate
I kissed some of my mates.
One kissed me.
The new manager doesn't understand.
He calls us 'poofs'.

He says it's not good
For my career.
Now I'm moving to Arsenal.
I want to come out.
The manager seems more enlightened,
Not like those 'old farts' at the FA.
They're holding us back.
It's okay to be a gay
Basketball player, rugby player,
Swimmer, tennis player,
Diver, whatever.
I talk to my agent.
He's against it: bad for business.
I decide to talk to the press
Nonetheless.
I make it short and sweet:
No scandalous stories to tell.
I inhale, exhale and stand:
'Ladies and gentlemen,
My name is Jasper Jay.
I love…
Scoring goals.
AND I'M PROUD
TO BE GAY…'
It's not been easy,
But now I hope other players
Will come out too.
This is for Justin Fashanu…

Soon after Rosa died, I went to pieces for a bit, and one day at Uncle Franco's I took nine Paracetamol. I was only trying to feel, I mean fill, that void of emptiness, that ache of hollowness I experienced when she died and I still hadn't cried.

I confessed to Auntie Doreen. She said I hadn't taken enough to do any harm. Subconsciously I knew this. During that time in Barnet, life for me was as alien as the planet Mars. They even had a bloody swimming pool, but I was never that keen on swimming. I missed the familiarity of Dorset Street, the inner London environment, even though I knew things would never be the same.

Damien tried to cheer me up by introducing me to smoking dope. I liked grass rather than hash, but I wasn't a smoker and couldn't get the hang of drawing on a pipe so never pursued it for long. Only when I was with him would I have the occasional puff. The funniest time I remember was him taking me to a Henri Matisse exhibition. I think it was at Tate Britain. Smoking grass made me laugh and we were both giggling as we entered the gallery

I was saying 'I love Matisse, he's my favourite painter.'

Damien was saying that Matisse was always in turmoil. 'Painting was agitation.'

I creased up at this. I couldn't stop saying 'Painting is agitation, painting is agitation' in a Dalek voice.

Apparently Matisse said that in order to begin painting at all, he needed to feel the urge to strangle someone or lance an abscess in his psyche, and that's when he started doing more decorative pieces…

When I got back from my sojourn in East Anglia I wanted to move back to Dorset Street. I discussed it with the priests from the Polish church who said I could keep the flat on until I found somewhere else. They had already decided that it was a good opportunity for them to stop renting it out, modernise it and make the whole house into a proper educational establishment, a bit like my old school in Douglas

Terrace. By this time the Mad Priest had been sent to a religious retirement home – or the loony bin…

The money Rosa had left me finally came through, paid to me in a cheque by Uncle Franco's solicitor. It wasn't a massive amount but it was the biggest cheque I had ever received. I still have her pieces of jewellery. Have never known what to do with them.

I took some driving lessons, passed first time and bought myself, wait for it, a bubble car – an *Isetta*! Bubble cars became popular when fuel prices increased in the late fifties. Mine was a three-wheeler which meant I could tax and license it like a motorbike. They were first made in Germany. Britain gained the licence to build right-hand drive versions of the *Heinkel Kabine*, manufactured by former German military aircraft manufacturers, and the Italian *Isetta*, manufactured under licence by BMW, who I later discovered were the masters of enforced labour during the war.

It was fun for a while, but I felt slightly unsafe in it. And it was too small for Mungo.

'You can back in with this bubble car, but I need to get out first.'

'Backing the car? Whaddya mean, man?'

I nearly hit a parking meter once.

Mungo said: 'You missed it by an inch!'

'Mystic? And here's me stick!'

So then I bought a second-hand VW Beetle. It was perfect and I christened it Ringo.

When Mungo said that Yolanda had kindly offered me the empty flat above her provisions shop in Leather Lane, it was too good an offer to miss so I quickly said yes. Yolanda had to clear it out so the arrangement was for me to move there in a month or two. I started packing up my few meagre possessions and going through my mother's things. I had her death certificate but couldn't find her birth certificate. There were a few bits and pieces: stacks of letters, stuff about Piotr and a few photos packed into a white leatherette case. I didn't read any of it and only glanced at the photos. There was a gorgeous sepia one of a beautiful woman in Victorian clothes, holding a darker little girl in her lap. My grandmother and great-grandmother, perhaps. In the photos of Piotr, he looked different in every one. There was only one photo of Rosa and Piotr together on what I guessed was their wedding day. I packed everything back in the leatherette suitcase and forgot about it all…

Piotr's photos made me realise that we are all multi-personalities, even physically speaking. We look unreal in every photo, displaying our public persona. We are often one person in public, another in private. I have tried constructing a personality for myself: friendly, charming, chatty, but my deafness holds me back. I will never be any of these things. Then I wonder if I would have been different if I'd had a brother or a sister like Clarrie, or even a twin. On the other hand, it must be very disturbing, even tiresome, seeing an identical-looking person all the time.

When Uncle Franco died a few years ago of a heart attack we all crowded into the Italian church for the funeral. Many people attended, unlike Rosa's funeral where there had only been a handful of people. All his friends, relatives, business acquaintances and many customers from the restaurants came, even strangers. Cousin Frank and his family came all the way from Australia. When Uncle Vince walked in late through the side door, it gave me a huge shock. For a few seconds I had forgotten he and Uncle Franco were identical twins. It was like Uncle Franco was still alive, walking into the church to attend his own funeral. Weird.

Journey North to South

I was in Venice
With an old acquaintance
Jolly and affectionate.
Arm around my shoulders
We travelled underground
In a stone-age lift
Exploring this nether lost paradise
A beautiful world of elegant hotels
And top-notch restaurants.
We kissed lingeringly,
Holding tight against each other,
Our passion heightened,
We were complete.
No longer the empty vessels
We had become.
Then we were away again
Upwards in the cavernous lift
Back to ground level. Next
We planned to go to Rome.
But I had lost my wallet
And had to travel back,
Plunging down in the rattling cage.
I couldn't find it and joked
That you would have to pay
For everything on our trip.
You stopped smiling then.
Our love forever broken.

I was looking around for a new job and found one pretty quickly as an office window cleaner in the city. And I enjoyed it. I'm not great with heights but I managed it. The cradle seemed pretty secure and I didn't mind the tedium of cleaning large expanses of glass. I actually gained immense satisfaction from seeing the clean bright glass. I wasn't skilled enough to use the very long brushes so at first I was allocated the shorter windows to clean. Then one day I arrived at one narrow Victorian office building and the janitor asked if I could clean the insides as well as the outsides of the windows on the top floor. Again it wasn't my job to do this but I agreed without thinking much more about it. So I started to clean the two sash windows from the inside. Nearly all the girls in the typing pool stopped clacking away on their typewriters and watched me. I felt embarrassed. Wearing my updated hearing aids, I could hear virtually every little noise, even the electric typewriters, so the silence was quite unnerving. I finished the windows as best I could with the chamois leather and beat a hasty retreat. But then I noticed that one of the windows needed a clean on the outside as well. Jake, the guy in the cradle outside, must have missed it by mistake. So I opened the window and sat on the ledge facing inwards and reached upwards. I caught the eye of one of the typists who winked at me.

Next thing I remembered was waking up in hospital. I'm still not quite sure what happened. When Jake visited me he said he had jumped out of the cradle as he guided it to the ground floor. As it was swaying a bit he straightened it. As he looked up he heard a scream. It was me, falling out of the top floor window, like a sky-diver. He thought I was a goner, but rather than crashing to the ground I landed on the roof of a car parked outside the office block and that saved my life. I was in a coma for several days, and when I woke up I had numerous broken bones and my hearing seemed even worse.

I was on state benefits for a while and I didn't feel like driving. Even though I couldn't remember it, I felt foolish having landed on the roof of a car. I had made a huge dent in it and obviously the owner wasn't a happy bunny. The window cleaning company said I shouldn't have been leaning out of the window in the first place as it was against safety regulations, but Uncle Franco got some personal injuries lawyer on the case. There were umpteen insurance forms to fill out and eventually I was given some compensation.

When I was still in hospital, Mungo, who visited every day said I needed a holiday and that he would pay for everything. All I needed was some pocket money. I couldn't think of any objection so we drove to Italy in his VW camper van.

I could write a travelogue, but not like hers...

We crossed the Channel on a ferry from Dover to Calais. Mungo had driven to Italy a few times before but it was my first time driving on the continent. He did most of the driving but I occasionally took over on the dual carriageways so he could have a snooze. I kept at a steady sixty, always keeping to the inside lane if I could, unless I overtook another extremely slow vehicle or lorry. The van had no great acceleration in any case and I enjoyed driving at a steady pace. We travelled through Burgundy to Dijon where we stayed just outside in a campsite. French sites are amazing, all mod cons. French people bring their TV, plants, pets, kitchen sink, home from home. Mungo's idea was to follow the old pilgrimage route down to Rome, and then on to Naples, Calabria, and even Sicily, if we had time. Then we would drive back up the other side to Vieste, Ancona, Rimini, Venice, and from there take the motorways back to Blighty.

After we crossed the Alps at the Mont Blanc tunnel we arrived in Italy via Val d'Aosta. Mungo said he was heading for Lunano where he had relatives, and I realised it wasn't that far from the village where my great-grandmother had originated. This was an area of huge emigration in the late nineteenth and early twentieth century, so quite a few British Italians hailed from this region and it was part of the original pilgrimage route. I persuaded Mungo to take a short detour to Torretta (on one of the subsidiary pilgrimage routes for people who wanted to reach Rome by climbing over the mountains, which was perceived as more spiritually uplifting than walking in the flat plains). I wasn't very impressed at first as we passed a massive cement factory, but after that the valley spread out and snow-capped mountains appeared in the distance as we drove alongside an impressive lake. We continued to climb up and up until we reached the turning for Torretta. It's quite a remote village at nearly 500 metres above sea level. We didn't stop long, but it's a pretty little spot, with many of its medieval houses restored and renovated. It overlooks the lake and is surrounded by vineyards and the distant Alps to the north. I discovered the lake was artificial, a dam built by Mussolini in the late twenties and used to irrigate the lower plains of the Po Valley.

Rosa had spent one holiday in Torretta as a young child before the Second World War but she had never talked about it. I found it quite captivating and would have liked to stay longer. We took our leave before dusk as Mungo was keen to make tracks. Before leaving I had gone for a walk by the side of the *fontana* – the spring. In the distance I could see the old church ruins silhouetted against the purple sky and the black outline of bats, those early pioneers of flight, soaring about. I instinctively ducked my head as they whizzed past. And now it's sad that even bats are in danger of extinction.

We had dinner with Mungo's cousins in Lunano. They begged us to stay the night with them but we ended up at a campsite on the Via Emilia, and early next morning we started the long drive down south. The dual carriageways were filled with lovely flowers and shrubs like oleander, or even a few orange and lemon trees the further south we went.

'What are those large flowers?' I asked Mungo, pointing to a wonderful display.

'Peonies. Red peonies.'

'Red penis? Where?'

The next night we stopped in a campsite on a hillside overlooking Florence, or *Firenze*, with the domed cathedral and the other Renaissance buildings theatrically lit up in the evening sun. I recollect the myriad flashing fireflies – *lucciole,* as Italian prostitutes are called – illuminating the dark silence below the moonlit starry sky.

Next morning Mungo stupidly left one of his many rings in the gents' shower room, but amazingly when he reported it at the campsite office, someone had handed it in. We couldn't believe that such honesty still existed in Italy, of all places. We stayed a couple of days visiting museums and churches. My favourite was near the station, *Santa Maria Novella* with its Giotto and Ghirlandaio frescoes. The whole of Florence was a delight, even if it was filled with Brits, Yanks and Germans... and I even managed to keep to my veggie diet without too many problems: 'Niente carne', which they seemed to understand. From Florence we headed to Rome and did the usual tourist stuff. Rome was magnificent, every road from the largest to the narrowest piled with buildings from different periods of history. Sighting the Pantheon and walking around the Forum with its Judas trees are both particularly impressive memories, not to mention the numerous fountains popping up everywhere. St Peter's was majestic but rather too baroque for my taste. When we walked down the nave, someone who looked like the fat chap in *Clink* or Roland the astrologer was showing a very beautiful young man the massive marble altar. How could anyone have sex with that rolling mass of fat? The young man was very attractive, but I despised him for being with such a person... I don't get this 'beautiful young men with fat old farts' syndrome. Surely it can't just be for money, or is it? The other thing that disgusted me was the foot on the black marble statue of St Peter situated near the exit. The whole foot has been worn away because of people continually touching or stroking it, or even worse kissing it. It seemed anachronistic, even pathetic, to me. It wasn't a real saint, just a very uninspiring black marble statue.

We liked Trastevere where there were some very reasonably-priced *trattorie*. I mean really cheap. This was the latter part of the eighties and you could still get a meal for less than a fiver – in Rome! I kept to pasta with tomato sauce, *penne con salsa di pomodoro,* which I spiced up by adding a little chilli or paprika to it, usually to be found on the table or on a sideboard in any restaurant. The salads were interesting, really varied. We had thistle salad once, which I nearly choked on at first but it was surprisingly tasty. And the ice cream was just fabulous, so much better than any English variety. The campsite we stayed in was a bus ride away from the centre, and after three days visiting Rome we headed to Ostia which was quaint and less crowded than I expected. We even managed a swim. I'm not a great swimmer and try to keep within my depth, but Mungo steamed off towards the horizon like a train. The undercurrent was very strong and the water got very deep almost immediately. I managed to float on my back for a while but then I struggled to turn over, and even though I was very close to the beach I couldn't haul myself up in time before being knocked over by an enormous wave! For a few seconds I experienced a drowning sensation with water flooding my eyes, nose and ears. It was like being flushed out by a water cistern, cleansed and purified. A Roman baptism, in fact. I finally managed to squeeze all the water out of my eyes and ears... and the snot out of my nose...

From Ostia we took the motorway to Naples. Mungo was getting excited. His mother's family were Neapolitan. His dad's family were Russian Jews from the Ukraine, but he knew little about them. Rather like my family background really. Naples was bustling and crazy, speeding cars not stopping at red traffic lights and guys hurtling past a millimetre away from us on scooters. We knew to keep our money well hidden but we never encountered any crime, just swarms of police storming around carrying loaded pistols and machine guns or police cars racing by, sirens screaming... I suppose robberies were happening all the time, we just never noticed them. Too busy eating pizza and ice creams and drinking the wine. I have never been a great drinker but I *was* on holiday. Mungo and I always shared half a litre of red with our meals, lunchtime and dinner. Not being used to red wine, I got drunk quickly. After lunch we headed back to whatever campsite we were in to sleep it off in the hot afternoons. The campsite in Naples was high up above the bay, and we had a wonderful view of Vesuvius, which looked as if it were erupting! I could imagine it bubbling up violently and devastating the surrounding area with its lava like it did in AD79.

From Naples we drove down to Sorrento, and had a quick visit to Pompeii and Herculaneum on route. Pompeii was awesome, all those bodies covered in ash, and I especially liked the naughty frescoes. Herculaneum was even better because you could really imagine it as a town and people living there. I could have spent hours there, but Mungo was keen to move on to Calabria where my Nonna Angela had come from. We headed to the A23, signposted Reggio Calabria. There were no tolls so it wasn't a motorway, but it was in an endless process of being modernised and upgraded. There was obviously a long way to go. Enormous new tunnels were being built so we had to use the service tunnels instead. Whole chunks of road seemed to disappear, and we avoided these chasms by using the narrow single lane contraflows. At one point we had to negotiate a very long single-track lane on one part of a two-tier section, with the other yet-to-be-repaired carriageway dangerously suspended above us. There was no way to get off and our patience was severely tested, not to mention having to confront all the rude, reckless drivers we encountered. Not only their usual braking before indicating and speeding right up behind us, but trying to force us off the road when it was only one lane, or overtaking on a single lane and getting back in millimetres in front of us. It was utter hell and drove me completely crazy. I screamed once as I really thought some idiot was going to crash into us. Even Mungo looked worried and kept to the slow lane when we finally got back onto the dual carriageway. Things calmed down after that as the roadworks ceased for a while. The, suddenly, a stray dog appeared on the road, causing further chaos. A police car started stalking him but the policemen were making no attempt to catch the poor thing, a bedraggled brownish-grey retriever, jaw hanging, drooling or foaming. We thought it could be rabid. What a journey!

We learnt later that the road works had been going on for years, and the Mafia, or the 'Ndrangheta as they are called in Calabria, were siphoning off government funds.

All the huge piles of rubbish everywhere in Calabria were shocking too. There was a refuse strike which had started in Naples but had spread all over the south of Italy, and it was dragging on because of the Mafia behind it. It was abhorrent as I am a real recycling fiend, but surprisingly I grew accustomed to it after a couple of days.

We took it easy in Calabria and didn't drive too far in case we became entangled in more roadworks. We made our base in a camping village near Tropea. First night we ate at the only restaurant open outside the campsite. No other customers except for us, but pasta in a lemon sauce was surprisingly good. I even ate some fish. Not cheap, I seem to remember. We drank a whole litre of local white plus beers (we needed it!) and staggered back to the campsite. Next day we walked to Capo Vaticano along the road and then back along the beach. For lunch we drank some '*Brunello di Montalcino*' we bought in a supermarket on the road to the campsite at bargain price. Barely drinkable, obviously a fake label and a Calabrian scam no doubt.

When we arrived in Calabria we had passed many signs for 'San Mango' or '*Santu Mangu*' in Calabrian dialect, so Mungo guessed that this was the Italian for Mungo. I started calling him 'Old Fruit' for the rest of our trip.

I have done some further research on the '*Ndrangheta*, whom I find fascinating. Like the masonic society, it is highly organised and part of the Calabrian way of life. Although they have medieval origins involving deep-rooted rituals and a concept of the family as sacred, they are very effective and make more profits than many huge conglomerates.

Legend has it that all three branches of the Italian Mafia were founded in 1412 by three knights from Spain: Osso, Mastrosso and Carcagnosso. They fled Spain after committing a heinous crime. They hid in Favignana, a small island off Sicily, where they remained for twenty-five years, during which time they wrote the code of the 'honourable society'.

Osso subsequently founded the *Cosa Nostra* in Sicily. Mastrosso founded the '*Ndrangheta* in Calabria and Carcagnosso founded the *Camorra* in Campania.

The so-called *tree of knowledge*, found in a valley of Calabria, represents the organisation of the *'Ndrangheta*, i.e. the trunk, branch, twig, flower and leaf. The leaves that fall and rot on the ground represent the *'infamous traitors'*.

The *Capocrimine* is the *'Ndrangheta* crime chief. He leads the three Calabrian precincts or zones, which are organised around family and kinship groups, and who form the backbone of each zone.

The *Picciotti,* who do the dirty work, began to appear at the end of the nineteenth century. They were the 'cool geezers' or 'wide boys' of their day, with tattooed hieroglyphs on their arms, their tight flared trousers worn over pointed shoes, silk scarves with fluttering ends and hair in butterfly-quiffs. I could fancy myself dressed like one of them...

The *Picciotti* duelled with knives and slashed faces with razors. They punished betrayals or failures by covering victims with urine and faeces. Their bullying tactics undermined the sense of community and replaced it with fear.

Plus ça change. Saint Sebastian's had its fair share of bullies. Bullying thrives; it makes the world go round... In fact, the word *'Ndrangheta* derives from 'manliness' or 'heroism' in the Greek dialect spoken in the Bovaro district, which is where the writer Corrado Alvaro hailed from. He was one of the first journalists courageous enough to write about them.

In the past, several earthquakes and land erosion ensured there was no prosperity in Calabria, so crime prospered instead.

So I learnt that the *'Ndrangheta*, or 'Hydrangeas' as Mungo calls them, are really rich and powerful, and the most secretive and successful of the Italian Mafia involved in criminal activities all over the world. Not only prostitution, drugs and human trafficking, but also disposing of toxic or radioactive waste. In *The Guardian* recently it said they are sending vessels to Somalia and other developing countries filled with toxic and radioactive waste, which is either sunk at sea or the waste buried on land. The ban on illegal waste dumping has led to a lucrative business for them. The article said they make more profit than McDonald's, and also invested in the Far East long before anyone else. And they aren't just operational in the south but have a northern stronghold around Lombardy and Emilia-Romagna.

Mungo said: 'Bloody typical that Berlusconi and other politicians have turned a blind eye to their money-laundering, trafficking and murders.'

They are involved in banking as well as investment scams; they influence political and economic decisions, interfere in the health service and other public offices, orchestrate business exhibitions and fairs, and threaten anyone involved in anti-mafia investigations.

'So it's not just the South they control. And everyone seems powerless to stop them, the bastards,' I said to Mungo.

We met someone in that first restaurant who admitted that he was part of the 'Ndrangheta brotherhood. We saw him handing what looked like an innocuous packet of cigarettes to the owner, but Mungo reckoned it was filled with cash. Mungo managed to have a frank chat with him, which he roughly translated to me as:

'I am a blood brother of the orange tanga (*tanga arancia*).'

I thought he said the 'orangutanga'!

He meant the orange tanga fraternity in Calabria.

Today, the Calabrian countryside, with its olive trees and vineyards, seems deceivingly tranquil and unspoilt, yet under the surface dreadful, covert things are happening.

What really shocked me was that some of these gangsters are hiding in tunnels under the roads to avoid prosecution. No wonder the road works never get finished! These tunnels are called *malandrine*. They are special bunkers for *mafiosi* who need to hide out. I saw a photo of one in *The Guardian*. It was situated in the mafia-ridden town of Rosarno which we briefly passed through, also full of roadworks I seem to remember. A *malandrina* (singular) is fitted out with comfortable furniture and modern equipment, but I imagine being holed up like that would send you absolutely barmy. The irony being that as they are so like prison cells, these mafiosi may as well be in regular prison above ground. At least they would get some exercise.

One historical story I read concerned a witness in a mafia trial murdered by the *Picciotti*. He was lured to his death by the promise of goat meat. And then he got butchered like a goat.

Every September there is the Festival of Madonna of Polsi which is used as a cover for the *'Ndrangheta* bosses' annual meeting. There is obviously a big connection between religion and crime here, with the bribes being used to pay for religious feasts.

I wonder if organised crime flourishes even more when doctrinaire regimes are broken, for example the Mafia weren't so strong under Mussolini. And with the break-up of the Soviet Union the Russian mafia must be just as powerful now as its Italian equivalent. Some old boy we met in a bar said when communications with the rest of Italy improved after the building of the railway from the north to Calabria, this also led to increased crime and extortion. On top of that, he said, electoral reforms allowing more independent local government and increasing voting rights gave more opportunities for local political corruption and violence.

In spite of this menacing, mysterious, somewhat invisible criminal element, I loved our time in Calabria. On a clear day we could see Mount Etna and the Aeolian island of Stromboli. Oregano, which tasted so much better here, and pink columbine, and blue, red and yellow wild flowers were ubiquitous. Apart from the rubbish, it was stunning.

Me: 'In Italian, *compagna* is country or countryside, *campagno* is friend, right?'

Mungo: 'Nah! *Tu sei il mio compagno di scuola* but *la campagna è bella.*'

The beaches are all quite different, some long and sprawling, others set in coves or little bays. After that first night out, we bought produce from the surrounding local markets and I got quite good at cooking pasta with tomatoes, peppers, aubergines or asparagus and the famous spring onions of Tropea on the camper stove. Even Mungo refrained from meat. Who needs it when there are all those wonderful vegetables and delicious fruit on offer?

Mungo originally planned to get the ferry to Messina in Sicily, but in the end he changed his mind and we crossed over to the Adriatic and journeyed up the other side of Italy, stopping off near Bari one night. It looked like a fairytale scene with its white-plastered squat houses and church domes amidst a navy blue sea. We didn't go to Alberobello but we did see several *trulli* – the stone shepherd huts Alberello is famous for – on the road, and the beautiful peninsula of Vieste in Puglia where we stopped next. When we looked out of the van in the morning we could see the sea on all sides. Then the long haul up through Ancona and Rimini, stopping in Bologna, the red city, somewhere I felt really at home.

The red city
Sparkling light,
Red ochre,
Sunshine smiling
On the stout porticos.
Moving with
A happy grace,

Joking with taxi drivers,
Laughing and chatting
With waiters or waitresses,
Welcoming warmth
Wholeheartedly encouraged.
On that glorious day
Sitting by Santo Stefano
Balanced precariously
At a table on
The cobbled stones,
Slowly sipping Prosecco.
Our conversation mingles
With that of passers-by
And the brilliant blue sky.
The Romanesque magnificence
Of the church is
A suitable backdrop
For music.
I play Chopin
Nonchalantly on the piano
Against a yellow ochre curtain,
Georges Sand highlighted
In burnt sienna.
Nothing is tangible,
We are all shadows
Devoid of crude
Unsubstantiated passions.
Love can be old.
Yet we are still attracted,
By youth,
Beauty, art
And words of love...

Mungo was getting itchy feet. He wanted to get back to his shop. I wanted to go to Venice, but he said it would be difficult to drive the camper van into the city and parking there would cost a fortune, so we headed back home, this time going through Switzerland and Germany, crossing into France via Strasbourg. The tolls on the French motorway cost a bomb, but it was a doddle. There was barely any traffic on the roads, but perhaps just as expensive as parking in Venice, I thought to myself. We *sailed* through to Calais and caught the last ferry back that night.

Killing Berlusconi

No sex please…
An Englishwoman fell in love
With a Polish man.
She was fun but skittish,
'No sex please,
I'm British.'
The Polish man loved
The Englishwoman,
But he was no Latin lover,
'No sex please,
I want to be British.'
The woman tried a different tack
Without knowing the right moves in
The game of love and kisses,
'No sex please,
We're playing tennis!'

Mungo saved me. I relied on him. He made telephone calls for me when I couldn't bear to hold the telephone to my ear. I never could get used to putting the earpiece against my hearing aid, so always yanked out the aid to answer the phone. I still hate phones, especially mobile ones. I have trouble keying in the numbers, and they always need to be recharged, regardless of how often I use them.

Mungo also 'interpreted' for me when I couldn't hear other people speak. He often came shopping with me so that he could explain what shop assistants or supermarket cashiers were saying.

His sister Yolanda saved me too. I lived in her spare flat on a peppercorn rent and just had to pay the utility bills. She paid the rates, or council tax as it's presently called. She hadn't had much time to spring-clean it, but she'd got rid of all the junk and boxes she'd stored there.

At school we were called Laurel and Hardy because Mungo was short and fat and I was taller and thin. I hated it but Mungo thought it was a laugh. I always thought the boys were saying 'Harvey' and not 'Hardy'. People said I resembled Laurence Harvey. He of *Room at the Top…* or *The Manchurian Candidate.* Have I mentioned this before?

Am I celebrity crazy? Or obsessed with who is gay and who is not? There was always talk about Laurence Harvey. Gay men sometimes marry gay women, such as Harold Nicolson and Vita Sackville-West, to have children or for companionship. There are numerous others but I could get done for liable, I mean libel. I met Harold 'Kim' (after Kipling's Kim) Philby, once when I was working for Uncle Franco in Oxford Circus. Well, it looked like him, and he stared at me, touching my wrist as he held out his hand for the meagre chocolate ice cream I had scooped out for him. If he had come in again, maybe he would have recruited me. I too could have ended up working for the Russians. Then I would have become appalled by the present exploits of Putin, been condemned and executed in a faked suicide like that guy Berezovsky, found in his bathroom.

Mungo was short, squat and stubby (alliteration again, and why not?), rather similar to Stubby Kaye in *Guys and Dolls* except Mungo had thick brown curly hair, usually combed back over his forehead. He was clever but not academic and became a very successful jeweller with his own shop in Hatton Garden. He wore gold-rimmed square spectacles and copious gold jewellery – all 22-carat – mainly rings and a couple of bracelets, and, of course, his Rolex. Except for his taste in clothes and jewellery, we had lots in common, and he and I just clicked. Mungo had this feel of easy domesticity about him. He loved food and wine, was a great raconteur, and although we were the same age, he became the father figure I'd never had.

Mungo helped me move in Yolanda's spare flat. We had a fry-up first in the nearby café. It was set out like a buffet on heated metal stands and I helped myself to eggs, beans, mushrooms, tomatoes and chips. Mungo had everything: bacon, sausages, black pudding, fried bread, the whole works. After we finished we went back to Dorset Street and loaded up his car. It hardly took any time to get back to Leather Lane.

Mungo climbed the stairs loaded with my boxes of books and a few pots and pans and he started panting really heavily. I thought he was having a heart attack.

Mungo: 'I took too much.'

'Yeah, you talk too much.'

'I meant I took too much food to eat. I'm stuffed! Climbing those stairs with all these boxes really winded me. I have lots to do today, so I can't stay long.'

'Sorry, what?'

'I have to go back to my shop soon. I'll have to leave you to get on. If I were you, I'd be rushing around trying to get this place in order. You, though, think things through. Dorek, the philosopher.'

'Philosopher? I know what things?'

'You take your time, think about where things should go…'

'Nah, I don't…'

'As James Cagney says, I smell a rat. Hope you haven't got them in here, or mice…'

'What did you say, you're in a rut? Aren't we all?'

At this point Mungo says: 'You're getting worse, you're fucking deaf as a post.'

'What? Death as a post?' I laugh. 'I'm joking. I heard what you said.' Sometimes I misunderstand consciously and say 'what' without thinking, or I'm just not concentrating on what people say.

'I make guesses a lot of the time. I get by. I reach the right words, eventually…'

'You really must get down to that hospital and get yourself some new hearing aids.'

After I fell on that car I often forgot to put them in. I never really got used to wearing them. They felt overlarge and cumbersome. I was always trying to pull them out and they made my ears itch. I found I could manage most of the time without them. As long as people were facing me I could lip-read what they said.

'Yeah, I've been thinking about it. I'm guessing most of the time. Talking more about myself, interrupting people rather than listening to what they're saying. And now I formulate questions so that the answer can be either yes or no.'

'Yeah, I've noticed.'

'You're really good with me. You're so patient and you speak loudly and clearly. Not like certain others I know who mumble.'

'You mean Damien? But you know him…'

'I do him? I don't think so.'

'I said you *know* him. Damien, I mean, you know what he's like…'

'Yeah, I ask him a question and he can never answer "*yes*" or "*no*". He goes into one long diatribe or other, sometimes nothing to do with what I'm asking. His Nietzsche rantings, I call them.'

Mungo interrupted: 'What I'm trying to say, Dee, is it must be difficult being so deaf. Don't you feel isolated, lonely?'

'Yeah, of course, but I compensate. You know me: pretty stoical. I know I'm an outsider, strange almost to some people. Yes, I can feel isolated, a non-participant, a non-combatant in many ways, but I'm not sure it's purely to do with my deafness. Maybe I'm like this in any case.'

I didn't say this to Mungo, but my solitariness is more to do with that foolish obsession with Clarrie. Her failure to acknowledge me opened up this void in me, this emotional emptiness.

Instead, I said, 'Yeah, being deaf throws up all sorts of psychological problems. Some people can be rather unsympathetic, denying there's anything wrong with me, but as I said, you learn to be stoical. When I'm writing I love taking out my hearing aids, as they do make me feel uncomfortable and I enjoy my silent world.

'When I have to concentrate on listening to others it can be exhausting, and it's so hard to recognise where sounds are coming from, which I find very perplexing.'

'I reckon that deafness is a very complex disability, Dee mate, and I reckon you should go private.'

'Maybe. It looks like the NHS has given up on me in any case. I don't have to go for a check-up now until next December, plus they said it's too late to operate on my ears now. The bones are too diseased and all gnarled up like olive tree branches. I know opticians are now offering free hearing tests and digital aids.'

'Go to one then! Anyway I'd better go. I must get back to my shop. Ciao, Dee.'

'Okay, Mungo, dee you soon.'

I'm left standing in the middle of this huge space. It's about twice as big as our place in Dorset Street. One really big light room, a galley kitchen and a small bathroom with a shower; no bath, which I'm really pleased about. I prefer showers these days. This flat is great; it hasn't been lived in for years. I am tempted to leave everything as it is: all the cobwebs, the dust, the heavy furniture. There's even an upright piano here. I can have a tinkle on it, learn to play it. Why not!

I have a strange relationship with music. I love listening to it, love the sounds, the drama and the variations, but I am not musical. Even though I was taught to read music by the nuns and can play the recorder badly, I have never learnt to play the piano. I will try and teach myself. I might pick up a few tunes. I have never had a huge record collection. When I was young I bought a few 45s – Eddie Cochran, the Everly Brothers, Buddy Holly, even the Drifters, and then, of course, the Beatles and the Rolling Stones – but when I started wearing hearing aids, I stopped listening to music. Initially I found it too shrill, too loud, too disturbing.

These days I have digital hearing aids fitted with a programme for listening to music. I am more relaxed about it. I love guitar playing, ballet music, even opera, Handel, Mozart and Verdi, and my favourite is jazz, abstract and moody... Miles Davis on trumpet. I listen to it for hours... And I have always had a hankering to learn how to play the harp...

I love spiders. I could watch spiders spinning their webs, catching other insects, for hours. I don't like to disturb them. I always leave them on ceilings, windows, inside kitchen cupboards, in the bathroom shower. Why should they be killed? They are lovely creatures, doing their job, saving me the trouble of getting rid of other, nastier insects.

There was a double bed there already, a wardrobe, a settee, and a large oak table with four chairs. I used the table as my writing desk.

I still write avidly, even on this new PC. First, it was on my beloved Olivetti, sliding in the crisp white paper sheets, tapping away with all my might. It was odd when I found the metal carriage lever broken. I had no idea how it could have happened. It was if someone had done it deliberately.

I bought some new white linen bedding and some red cushions to use as pillows from the market. It was like a monastery, a spacious but spartan cell. It suited me well. My thoughts kept me company. I spent a long time blaming *her*, Clarrie, for my inadequacy, my sexual confusion, my inability to socialise with women. I was invisible to her even though I loved her, but I was confused about whether I wanted to be her or just love her as a separate person. I will never know what she thought. I can only know my own thoughts. I am in this body, no one else's. And what about me now? Here, now in this monk-like existence, flitting from one job to the next. Was I lonely because I wasn't in a relationship?

I would like someone to love. Someone who would call on me, care for me, write me love letters but people don't write letters any more. I haven't got used to typing emails on this new machine yet and I still don't understand the printer. It's so state of the art it looks like a time machine.

But I prefer email to the telephone, Facebook or Twitter. Take them or leave them.

Facebook is the new god,
Twitter the new confessional.
Prayer too outmoded,
Best to get things off your chest
Via social media.
Proclaim on Facebook,
Share your joys,
Sorrows,
Anger.
Tweet your indignation,
Or seek consolation,
Likes and shares
Better than
Godly intervention.
Celestial hyperspace,
Ego boosting
Internet religion.
Google the Father
Sony and
Holy Mac.

The main reason I went off Facebook was that out of the blue I got involved in correspondence with a *murderer* via a friend's post. There had been a pro-Roma demonstration which one of my Facebook friends had posted on his page, and that's how our 'communications' had started. This person – the murderer – was called Ivan Turnstone and was a member of the English Defence League. He was the friend of my friend, Johnny, who worked at Lincoln's Inn car park.

Ivan had replied to Johnny's post saying that the whole thing had started because three teenagers he knew had been blown up in their car by some gypsies. (Incidentally, this was never verified by the police. Apparently the car had been bought from a Roma site in Bedford. According to the police the brakes and gearbox had been tampered with.) Ivan reasoned that the gypsies had sold the faulty car deliberately so were ipso facto responsible for the boys' deaths (although he didn't express this in quite such terms).

I'm showing off! I've always wanted to use that expression. I do have moments of inspiration, eloquence, but at other times it's so difficult to write, to compose a good sentence.

As a quid pro quo he and his EDL friends had gone to the Roma camp to kill all the people living there. He said he hated gypsies, Roma, travellers, whatever they were called, and that they had no right to set up camp in English towns. He had simply got his revenge. After the camp was destroyed, a far-left group fire-bombed the EDL offices in Luton, but there was no one in the building at the time. It was like the start of civil war, and this was when I inadvertently got caught up in the Facebook correspondence.

Even though many people, not just me, abhorred the use of violence, it just spurred him on. I said nothing justified violence.

He said it was none of my business and I was naïve. He condoned violence when it was necessary. He believed that the Roma should not exist.

'There is no unfair treatment of them, at least not by me. These demonstrators will stand against me every chance they get. I am an upright law-abiding citizen. It's the gypsies who are filthy and trespass on our land.'

'Oh yes, very law-abiding, you have just demolished their camp and killed innocent children in the process. How can the needless (accidental or deliberate) slaughter of the Roma children in the camp be justifiable?'

'Dear Dorek, from what you wrote i [sic] understand

that you have no knowledge of gypsies, so please mind your own...Ta...'

'Nobody should mind their own business. The world has to progress and change. People like you spread hatred, spitefulness and the condoning of conflict.'

'Your judgment [sic] is so naive and wrong. I feel sorry for you. We were defending ourselves and upholding our rights! your argument is so dated...!

'If I were religious I would pray for you, my son...'

'Do not bother.'

Then a couple more people piped up with pro-Roma propaganda links and Ivan the Terrible asked his friend:

'Johnny, why do [...] let them use your facebook for propoganda [sic]? block them.'

It was the most ludicrous yet scariest thread I have ever seen on Facebook. Johnny tried to counter with a reasonable line of argument.

'Johnny, the violence started with three youngsters being killed...'

Unfortunately there will always be nationalistic and inhumane 'Tit for tat' or 'An eye for an eye' retaliations. Roma are unpopular and no 'nimby' wants them setting up camp nearby, but this is no justification for violence. Discussion and compromise, yes; annihilation, no. But it was very upsetting for me that people like Ivan thought he had a perfectly justifiable case and happily pronounced his intolerable views on Facebook.

Another reason I could never be a Catholic priest is having to hear the confessions of major criminals, rapists and murderers like Ivan. Nor do I wish to listen to fanatics on either side of the political spectrum. Sometimes it's good to be deaf.

As I have never lived with anyone apart from Rosa, I'm used to my own company; doing things the way I like;

not having to consider others; not having to compromise. I can fart when I want, eat garlic, let my breath smell. Never kissing. Never having sex with anyone. No intimacy, full stop.

What a nightmare trying to write this: I am frustrated; I can't get the words out.

I am not used to this new keyboard. I miss my Olivetti! The mistakes I make drive me mad. I'm unlucky being both asexual and deaf. I wonder if the two are connected. I don't think so, but obviously both have affected my life. I have finally admitted it. I am doubly disabled. No hearing, no sex. But I have grown accustomed to this. I don't need conversations, flirting, grappling, taking off clothes. Sex is messy, squalid, and as I have never really experienced loving or passionate sex, I can't think otherwise. Socialising out of sexual motivation is not me. No need for me to pay for meals, hotels or holidays. Joe Orton hated that too, but for a different reason. All he wanted was sex, whereas I don't. Sometimes I would like a hug, to be cuddled. But this is a craving for affection, not sex. Enough ranting now.

Another fantasy of mine is about Silvio Berlusconi: rich, slimy, greedy bastard. When that guy hit him with that statue of Milan cathedral, how I cheered and guffawed (I like this word!). Yet it could have been a put-up job to get the sympathy vote or because he needed more plastic surgery.

Killing Berlusconi

I am dying, so why not do something outrageous? Kill a well-known hate figure.

I have always loathed Berlusconi and wondered how a majority of Italians could have voted for him in three elections. One cousin I asked said as he was rich he wasn't in politics to make money!

'Ha, ha! Don't make me laugh,' I said, 'the complete opposite is true.'

He monopolised the media and changed parliamentary laws to suit his own ends. His wealth quadrupled while he was in power. I suppose the problem was that because he controlled the media, even state television channels RAI (they run commercials but you also pay a licence fee), many people, even intelligent ones, voted for him. I still couldn't understand it though.

It's like electing Rupert Murdoch to be Prime Minister. The Murdochs have enough power as it is, but I'm sure it couldn't happen here. A media giant becoming a politician and fixing the law to make himself invincible? As for all that bunga bunga and underage sex, many Italians thought it was a laugh and condoned it. If I lived in Italy I would have taken a pop at him, like that guy who threw the statue at him. Either the guy was just a loony, or the luscious Silvio orchestrated the whole thing because he had to go into hospital for a while for another operation to fix his face: more hair weaving or more Botox or liposuction and the rest.

If I were a terminally ill Italian cancer patient, it could have gone like this: Google when he's going to be at a public meeting in an accessible town. Wear a mac or heavy coat with inside pockets. Carry a flick knife in one of the pockets and/or a bottle of acid, or other disfiguring agent. I would have fought my way through the crowds, jostled into position and somehow eluded his bodyguards. They never seemed to be concentrating that hard on guarding him and were often laughing and joking in the television pictures I saw. And then, when I thought I had the right opportunity, I could either have stabbed him or covered him in acid. The problem being which one would I have chosen? A dilemma.

And then he got his comeuppance in any case, all those trials regarding illegal sex and fraud. He squirmed and wriggled and nearly succeeded in getting round the judges. They have finally banned him from being a senator and applying for a government position, but he can still campaign locally. He's too old to go to prison, but apparently he has to do public service at an old people's home four hours a week... and ironically... it's in the town where the statue-thrower came from! And his party, which has changed its name so many times I can't keep track, I think it's reverted to being called Forza Italia, is in total disarray, and his supporters are leaving in droves. So maybe I don't have to kill him now. But I still don't understand how a 77-year-old man, insincere and artificial in both body and soul, managed to wield so much power and con so many Italians. Obviously he paid everyone off to do his bidding. Perhaps every nation has the capability of breeding one monster sooner or later.

Ledder Lainer Life

The beauteous world
We live in,
Senses blasted,
Feelings heightened
To quasi hysteria,
Too much contradiction
For us to comprehend.
Nature inspiring,
Art sublime,
Creativity bursting
Amid blind panic.
And war, worryingly
Always war...
Women know it's wrong.
Our world's torn middle,
Unethical killings,
Blitz of illegal weapons,
A blot on Nature's
Bounteous landscape.
Senseless regression
Febrile feelings
Creativeness crushed
Helpless in inhumanity's
Vacillating wake.
Western intervention
No more the answer
Than sticking
One's head
In the sand.

Leather Lane was a great place to live. I enjoyed the hustle and bustle of the market, and every day I could buy fresh fruit and veggies and pop in to Yolanda's to get whatever else I needed. And when I was too lazy to go to the launderette, I just bought new underwear, socks or shirts off one of the market stalls. Hence I have quite a few clothes that could be recycled, once washed, of course.

The entrance to the flat was through a heavy door to the side of the shop. Burglar-proof, I thought. Yet when I got back from our trip to Italy, the flat looked different. Not in any overwhelming sense, but the bed had been made up differently, dishes and saucepans were stacked in a new order in the kitchen, and my books had been rearranged. Strangest of all there was a list of unrecognisable names in the telephone address book, and, of course, my broken Olivetti carriage return, but luckily no porridge eaten or chairs broken by Goldilocks. Nothing had been stolen and all the old brown furniture was still in place. It was then I decided I was going to spend some money on the place, modernise it and redecorate.

Then, alleluia, I got my dream job as a car park attendant at Lincoln's Inn, reporting to the Deputy Chief Porter and working the daytime-shift. The benchers, barristers, solicitors and other officials had annually registered parking permits. Those who didn't had to pay a daily rate. I had to oversee the various clients, contractors and other sorts who visited during the day and paid the same daily rate. In the evenings parking was free by application. The private residents and tenants with permits drove in or out at other hours of the day, but much of the time I was free to indulge my passion for reading in my wooden cabin near the gatehouse, or 'rabbit hutch' as I named it. The Lincoln's Inn library was open to barristers and students, and I always said I would apply to gain entry to the rare manuscripts displayed there, but I never got round to it. I only visited the Inigo Jones chapel and the often-redesigned Great Hall once the whole time I worked there.

Lincoln's Inn Fields housed the Royal College of Surgeons and various other institutions. My favourite place in the Fields was Sir John Soane's museum on the opposite side. The architectural drawings, paintings, and especially the sculptures, had a great effect on me. The Monk's Parlour and Yard in the basement was very spooky, teaming with gothic or Roman ornaments and heads. It was supposed to be a suite of rooms for an imaginary monk, 'Padre Giovanni', whose tomb is in the yard. In fact, it's the grave of Fanny, a dog belonging to Mrs Soane. The headstone is inscribed with the words 'Alas, Poor Fanny!' The crypt contains the sarcophagus of King Seti I of Egypt. I spent hours in there but wouldn't have liked to have been locked in down there after dark.

When I wasn't in the hut I enjoyed the fresh air, and as an employee I was allowed to play tennis doubles with Damien, Dino and Walter on one of the three tarmac courts. We all played at a leisurely pace except for Damien, so Dino, who was fitter than me, was always his partner. Walter and I were less competitive than the other pair and played for fun. I had a slow serve, which was surprisingly deceptive and which used to rile Damien when he missed it.

Every so often I felt restless again. I didn't know what I wanted from life. Sometimes it was like having agoraphobia, and when I wasn't working I didn't want to leave the flat. Then it was the opposite and I planned to travel around the world.

My new hearing aids, which I bought privately through *Glass Eyed* opticians, worked quite well. They were much neater than the NHS ones and required smaller batteries. In David Lodge's novel *Deaf Sentence* he advises that when replacing a battery you should take off the little cover protecting it and leave it for a minute before inserting it inside the hearing aid to make it last longer. Personally, I have never noticed much difference.

I started attending evening classes – literary appreciation, creative writing, that kind of stuff. I had this inexplicable ambition to write, but no one ever encouraged me. At the creative writing class at Holborn College, the teacher was called Julian March. He was so laid back he was bloody horizontal. His idea of teaching was to let us get on with it, even though the hand-out at the beginning of the term had led us to believe it was a very structured class with suggestions on how to get an agent or find a publisher. I don't think he ever mentioned the words 'agent' or 'publisher' the entire time I was there. Instead every week he made us read a piece of our work. I read some of my poems, but he was never very positive. The only short piece he liked was when I wrote about being deaf:

> *Writing is solitary, yet*
> *It gives me strength*
> *And helps me*
> *Forget I cannot*
> *Hear the world outside.*

I didn't show him my other piece:

> *Farting shitting or defecating peeing or urinating,*
> *Throwing up vomiting sneezing hiccupping,*
> *Picking your nose scraping ear wax out,*
> *Blowing your nose brushing or flossing your teeth,*
> *Going to the dentist having fillings teeth extracted*
> *What about sickies gagging,*
> *Coughing up those hard bits of what?*

I know they have a ghastly smell...
Do we write about this?
And do women write about menstruating?
Bloody accidents?
Dunno...

And it wasn't only me Julian didn't like. A Russian girl was writing a sci-fi novel, and all he could say about it was that it was 'too arty'. It was a very cleverly plotted book and the characters were believable and intense. I thought it was great, but he gave her no praise.

He was only interested in a woman called Nancy Martin. She was writing a thriller set in 'Dordogneshire' where the husband of the main character was poisoned by a wild mushroom. It was dire stuff and badly plotted as the killer was only introduced in the penultimate chapter, but Julian couldn't stop enthusing about it. I heard the other students in the class muttering that they were having an affair. Well, I did hear some of their strange banter, which went something like this:

Julian: 'I can't swim.'

Nancy: 'Really, I find that unbelievable. Everyone can swim.'

Julian: 'I don't have sex either.'

Nancy: 'Oh! Well, that I find more believable.'

Julian: 'What about the sex we had last night?'

Nancy: 'You promised you wouldn't mention that in class.'

They could have been joking, but she wasn't renowned for her sense of humour. But if they were having an affair, I couldn't work out what she saw in him. He was nondescript and lumpy with heavy, dark bags under his eyes, like a bulldog's, and he wore baggy mismatched clothes, mainly in dark colours but with an occasional odd dash of colour, like an orange polka-dotted scarf or floral lilac tie. He was obviously one of those people who 'teach' rather than 'do'. He'd had a few minor poems published, but nothing of any merit. I have always felt strongly about the teaching profession. Not all are mediocre or unsuccessful like him. He was the exception rather than the rule. The majority of teachers, especially in primary and secondary education, are very dedicated, and successive governments should stop interfering in their work.

The strange thing is, though, I dreamt about Julian:

Two-stage dream

Julian March and I met in an Oxbridge college quad, maybe Magdalen. Not sure exactly why we were there, possibly on an educational trip to see Hamlet at the Oxford Playhouse. Julian was saying that listening to dialogue of a play would help me with my own dialogue, but I was thinking that trying to listen to Shakespeare is not the same as trying to write vernacular everyday speech. I need subtitles to watch a Shakespearian play, or rather, surtitles... So I told him this, and then unexpectedly he blurted out:

'I want to make love to you. I'll even marry you...'

What had brought this on? I wondered. Julian gay, proposing gay marriage?

I must have woken up for an instant as I stopped dreaming, and what seemed much later on, during the night or even early morning, I dreamt that I replayed his words in my mind, thinking they were true. I was wondering how I would deal with him when I saw him next in class after his confession. I came to the decision never to return to the class. I wasn't getting much out of it in any case. I thought he was a lousy teacher, although he was very popular with some of the others.

So even though this was only a dream, I never did go to his creative writing class ever again.

Julian continually reiterated how important it was to 'show' rather than 'tell', but I must admit I never quite fathomed what this meant. When Rosa told me a story, she didn't show it. She didn't mime it. She did do voices, though…

I was lucky living in the heart of London. And after my window-cleaning accident I decided I didn't need a car. Psychologically, I think I must have been put off driving after falling onto that car. Besides, there was nowhere to park in Leather Lane.

Mainly I used buses, the 19 or 38, and sometimes the Holborn Tube, but often I walked. My favourite destinations were the National Gallery, the National Portrait Gallery, the Tate in Millbank and the Rembrandts in Kenwood House. I can stare at a Rembrandt for hours. All that character in his subjects' faces, their unusual poses. I know he was paid to do these portraits, but it's as if he was searching his sitters' souls. You can see inside them. I love the dark backgrounds and their beautifully painted hands. That woman bathing of his, with her sturdy yet voluptuous figure, is much more realistic, more tangible, than any Reubens.

My most favourite was the Courtauld Collection which used to be in Woburn Place. I loved the vibrant colours of the Impressionists, and the Omega Workshop stuff which I really coveted. I even took up pottery and threw a few pots. My minimalist flat became filled with brightly coloured painted misshapen vases, jugs, bowls, and enormous impractical cups and saucers, but they livened up my flat which I had painted totally white. I was also tempted to decorate the piano but never got round to it. I attempted some pencil drawings at another class. There was so much choice for evening classes in those days, especially in the Holborn area. My drawings consisted of very detailed black wavy lines and dots, and unlike my pots, never anything in colour. They looked rather good but I never got round to hanging them up.

One of my favourite painters is Van Gogh who cut off his ear. Not because of any brotherly ear sympathy I feel for him. I simply love his use of colour and the way the thick waves of paint look so fresh, as if recently applied to the canvas.

Another newly-discovered pastime was the theatre. There were quite a few schemes for the hearing-impaired and I went to all the captioned performances I could find. The National Theatre was best, and I enjoyed the walk over Hungerford Bridge seeing the most famous of London sites such as Big Ben, the Houses of Parliament and the Millennium Wheel spread out around me. And walking from St Pauls to the Tate Modern over the Millennium Bridge was exhilarating too.

The Thames has always fascinated me. I imagine it in Dickensian times: the rotting smells, the chaos, the boats and tugs, the mud, the inlets, the hiding places, the dead bodies floating downriver... It's the setting for a novel I read by Lesley Thomson, *The Detective's Daughter*. A female corpse is discovered floating in the Thames. This is much more dramatic than the real life event the book is based on, where an unfortunate young woman, with her young child present, was found murdered in Richmond Park.

Playing in the squidgy mud and inhaling the pungent oily smells. Sailing barges or refuse-laden boats nonchalantly tugging up and down, ignoring the secret immersed bodies... The odd bone white limb sticking out, floating torsos half undressed... Hidden crevices and secret beaches, pubs with jetties... the sweet aroma of spices around Butler's Wharf, the looming Tower Bridge... opening like a flower...

I took up photography for a while, developed my own pictures in black and white – influenced by the Italian realists' films I had watched as a boy – but I was never satisfied with any of them.

Jake's Joke

"For a very short time in the eighties, I worked as a temporary projectionist at a porn cinema in Kings Cross. It was called The Office Cinema, so guys could call their wives and say, 'I'm still at the office.'"

Actress dream

I am an actress, or training to be one. Unexpectedly and at the last minute I'm given a part in a production in an arts centre theatre club. I'm handed the script but have no idea what the play is about. I haven't attended any of the rehearsals and I find myself up on the stage in front of the live audience. A woman is in bed and there are two other actors besides me on set. I discover that the play is mainly improvised – loads of ad-libbing. The two men are disputing what the woman in bed is saying. They insist she's been having an affair, but she denies it. She says she has been spending time... doing ... I can't hear what she says, but I think she says 'solarium' or 'sun-tanning lounge'. So I say, 'Well, she doesn't look very tanned to me!' which gets the most enormous laugh from the audience.

I told Mungo (jokingly) that my ambition had always been to do PPE at Oxford.

'Why Oxford? You can do PE anywhere!'

'PPE is philosophy, politics and economics, you idiot… I could be a politician, you know. I would call my party *Climate Emergency*. Capitalism will collapse as the planet's resources dwindle and global warming increases. Children should be taught how to survive in this warmer world.

'Yeah, yeah, I was taking the mick. PE is something you would've said…'

I'm digressing again. What I intended to recount was my surprise discovery about the circumstances of my birth.

I was clearing up the Leather Lane flat after I had finished decorating. I had refurbished the entire flat and installed a new kitchen, with a little outside help. I finally went through the white leatherette suitcase containing all Rosa's papers, stored on the top of the wardrobe, to see what I could throw out. I couldn't find her marriage certificate. I did eventually find, however, Piotr's death certificate. He died in Camden, London, 10 March 1947. Over two years before I was born! There were several letters between him and Rosa. One mentioned a planned trip to Paris. He was stationed around Normandy and Brittany while she was nursing in Kent. It seems he got to England in September 1945 and then the letters stopped. From the death certificate and St Pancras coroner's report he had received multiple injuries in a car accident on the A2 just past the Blackwall Tunnel after suffering a heart attack at the wheel. He was 35. Maybe I was right all along. He *was* a spy and was killed for some misdemeanour. I slumped down on the bed for a while, numb from the shock of discovering Piotr was not my father after all. I frantically started searching the suitcase again and found a huge bunch of envelopes tied up in red ribbons. Each letter was on embossed paper headed '*Reginald George Leach*

MBBS, FRCS (Gen Surg), MSc (Cantab)' and always signed 'You are the love of my life, George'.

I gathered that Rosa assisted Reginald George Leach, a general surgeon at Dovington Cottage Hospital in East Anglia, in the two years before I was born. George mentioned his difficult, neurotic French wife called Dorothée and a son called Victor. She wouldn't divorce him, even though he said he was desperate to marry Rosa.

I gleaned that my mother left Dovington abruptly in early 1949 and returned to the Polish house in Dorset Street. She gave no reason to George, but she was pregnant with me. I was born on 9 April 1949 so I am George's son. I googled the name Reginald George Leach and found nothing, but I did find his son, Victor Leach, also a surgeon, who had retired recently. According to a local newspaper he'd had a mental breakdown and was forced to leave Colwich hospital. He wasn't on Facebook and I couldn't find any contact details for him so I left it at that.

My father could have been anyone. It was just he wasn't Polish as I had been led to believe. He was English, and I had an older half-brother called Victor. Reginald stayed with his unstable wife as 'she couldn't survive without me' but he supported us financially, sending a monthly cheque. Rosa fell out with her brothers not over money but because of me being illegitimate. I'd admired Rosa for being so financially independent, but she'd had help all along. I wondered why she hadn't told me the truth: to keep up appearances and the 'bella figura' or because she was ashamed? Everyone must have guessed I wasn't Piotr's child, so why this deceit? No one ever talked about my Polish side because there wasn't one! There is no evidence that the good doctor knew about my deafness. He stopped writing to her in around 1964 when I was fifteen, before I had all those hearing tests. That must have been when the monthly cheques stopped, so he could have died. I remember Rosa muttering something about 'tying our horns' or 'tightening the purse strings' and becoming more parsimonious.

The Pioneering Operation

Doctor Leach, famous surgeon, is about to perform a ground-breaking and pioneer operation – the 'audioloscotopy'. He has invented a new technique for curing hearing loss caused by otosclerosis. He will attempt to separate the fused-together ossicles – in layman's terms, the ear bones of the middle ear. They are the malleus (hammer), incus (anvil), and stapes (stirrup). The procedure requires great delicacy and dexterity. With his extraordinary skill and great patience, he completes the operation in less than two hours.

He sits by his patient's bed, holding his hand, waiting for him to wake from the anaesthetic.

'Dorek, my boy, can you hear me?'

'Yes, I can, Dad!'

Fanfare of trumpets...

I was sad that Piotr, whom I had imagined being so courageous in the Second World War, wasn't my father after all. I knew nothing about this Leach person and had no idea what he'd done in the war. He was most probably in the medical corps. I didn't feel any desire to search further. I have always been dubious about my gender and sexuality, and now the truth about my parentage has thrown my identity into doubt as well. Somehow I wasn't that surprised.

So what? I was not half-Polish. Yet because I grew up in that Polish house and went to the Polish church, part of me will always feel some 'Polishness', and I will continue to get upset when present-day Poles are rubbished by politicians and the media. It's ironic I'm a pure Englishman after all. Rosa was born here and my dad was British. The name Wiadrowski wasn't mine. Those little suspicions I'd harboured about being turned down for jobs, well at least that one in the Civil Service, because of my surname were futile as was all the vitriol I'd received after one of my forays into a Guardian comments page about the referendum in Scotland, saying that if I were Scottish I would vote yes. The original article was about 'celebrities' who were in favour and those who weren't.

"England seems to be a little bit lost – obsessed with immigration, obsessed with anti-European sentiment, all these negative things. Maybe it's just time to cast off and do our own thing." So said Stuart Murdoch of *Belle and Sebastian,* who said he is now voting yes.

I simply agreed with him. What was wrong with that? Can't I have an opinion? My user name is DWiadrowski – I suppose it was naïve of me to use my own surname. One very rude person told me to go back to Poland!

I am obviously pleased that UKIP didn't do well in London, not just because of my political views but because of my 'Italian-Polish' heritage. When you actually study the statistics, as the Elles always said the number of immigrants from the European Community is very low. All that UKIP press coverage, their candidates exaggerating the numbers and the threat of more to come, is so ridiculous. Worst of all, Nigel's poncy face displayed everywhere. Here's what I think:

Blank page in a homage to Laurence Sterne…

Living Wills

Boring denting for ballroom dancing
Fingerbowl for Tinkerbelle
Tower two for tattoo
Carry Galli for Tariq Ali
Villain tear for volunteer
Valley for volley
Marie for Murray
Hide for high
Exhibition for expedition
Tally Van for Taliban
Mervin for Merlin
Barking ham Palace for Buckingham Palace
Tell gravel for Telegraph
Syllabus for celebrations
Ad walls for Ed Balls
Car lorries for calories
Injured Terries for inventories
Berkeleys for Barclays
Use for lose
Alligator for navigator
Wayne seller for wine cellar
Counting his underwear
For counting is underway
Build for fill
Leer call for lyrical
Falling for fielding
Resident for president
Lacked for let
Run the but for won the vote

Mew trait for mutate
And a half for on behalf
Sir Macca for Sir Malcolm
Lord for lured
Rebels anchor for Radwanska (Polish tennis player)
Batman for that man (Gerry Adamists or Jihadists)
Juice towers or reduced hours?

The list is endless. My current favourite subtitle error while watching golf: "He's had all sorts of problems with his bum" when commentator said 'thumb'!

Or there's: 'I'd like to buy a sexy' instead of 'I'd like to buy a sofa', and I have seen 'sofa' being used for 'safer'. The mistakes are often corrected, but even so you should guess that 'sofa' is nothing like 'sexy'. And 'by sexual' for 'bisexual'? Surely there must be a better computer programme the news channels could use. I have stopped watching most television news. Subtitles like these really irritate me. I could do a better job myself and I'm deaf... Though I confess I still watch the occasional film or drama series on television. The subtitles aren't so bad. Recently I bought myself an iPad. I read the news on this instead. And I am concentrating on getting this book finished.

Making a living will is a very good idea. Mungo and I discussed it often. Even Rosa was in favour, but the darling didn't need it in the end. I think Euthanasia, or *Yoofanasia* as Mungo called it, is a good idea.

'Yoofanasia, my dear!'

'What's that? Everlasting youth? No thanks...'

Euthanasia should be incorporated into a legal statute. Yet I have a feeling it could all go wrong, and that's why it's neither simple nor easy to change laws. People could abuse it...

Abusing Euthanasia

Elsa and Tony Radcliffe were devoted to each other. They were pushing seventy and had decided they should definitely make their final wills and testaments before they completely forgot or were too gaga to do it themselves. They were childless, but Elsa had a niece in Canada so everything was going to her. They firmly believed in the right to die, and vowed to assist in each other's suicide if either of them got a terminal illness. They went to their local Islington solicitor to draw up their last will and testaments and compile letters of wishes, or living wills …

Tony was very hard of hearing, so Elsa said:

'Don't worry, I'll sort it all out with Ms Strickton, the solicitor.'

They finally put their signatures to all the documents, including their living wills. Basically the living will document read something like this: 'Regarding any future medical care and treatment, I wish that my husband/wife, my doctors and any other medical personnel, institution or authority in the event that I shall be unable to make my views known at any time will carry out my wishes as follows:

Do Not Resuscitate.

My life shall not be artificially prolonged, and no life-sustaining treatment shall be administered, if at any time my attending doctor, consultant or surgeon and one independent medical practitioner certify in writing that in their opinion:

I have a terminal, incurable or irreversible injury, disease or illness; or

I am permanently unconscious, comatose, in a persistent vegetative state with no reasonable chance of recovery, and

I am no longer able to make decisions regarding my medical treatment.

In the above circumstances I wish to die naturally and to receive only such medical treatment as will alleviate any pain or distressing symptoms so as to make me more comfortable, even if this has the effect of shortening my life.'

Elsa had always been a little crazy, and over the years had grown quite eccentric. As she had never had children, she was mad about animals, even insects and other creatures, and adored her pet, a King Charles spaniel called Ronnie. He had recently been put down, and Elsa suddenly decided she wanted to spend the twilight years of her life travelling the world. She had visions of visiting Africa, Australia, New Zealand, China, Japan; but there was one small problem. Tony, her husband, hated flying.

They always motored everywhere, and had enjoyed holidays in Scotland, the Channel Islands, Ireland, France, Spain and Italy. Even Germany, which Tony felt was a decidedly underrated country.

'I have no wish to travel to another continent, even aboard QE2, and that's final…'

Elsa couldn't get Tony to budge, so she was forced to decide on another course of action. She racked her brains about how to go about it. After undertaking copious research, she had an idea. Laxatives! She secretly added a large dose of Senna leaves into all the meals she cooked for Tony. She had gleaned the following information:

'Senna is an herb. Its leaves and its fruit are used to make medicine. The leaves are more potent than the pods. Senna contains many chemicals called sennosides. Sennosides irritate the lining of the bowel, which causes a laxative effect.'

Tony loved curries or anything spicy, so the texture of the Senna leaves didn't arouse any suspicions in him. Sometimes she ground them up in advance, preparing the sauce for his meal separately, saying she would just have an egg or salad for supper.

After a few weeks, Tony was in a dreadful state and was always in the bathroom. He had lost two stone and looked terrible. Elsa fussed over him, still serving him the Senna leaves in herbal teas as he couldn't abide curries now.

'This delicious herbal tea is good for you.'

She convinced him that he must have cancer.

'Darling, you're not getting any better. I have an awful feeling your symptoms indicate the big C. Let's get you to the doctor now.'

Tony hated all things medical, but even he realised there was something wrong so he reluctantly agreed.

Elsa urgently arranged an appointment with their GP. When they got to the surgery, their regular doctor was away. The appointment was with a locum.

'Hello, I'm Doctor Kalumba. But do call me Charlie.'

Elsa thought him very attractive. She liked a chat. Before long she discovered he was Ghanaian, lonely and hoping to return to his family home one day.

'I've always wanted to go to Ghana,' she said, giving Tony a furtive look, hoping he wasn't concentrating on what she was saying.

The doctor told Tony that it could be bowel cancer and that he would need several tests at the hospital. Tony hated hospitals and looked despairingly at Elsa. They both got up to leave.

Elsa told Tony to wait outside a minute.

'I'll have a talk to that doctor.'

She closed the door while Tony went back to sit in the waiting room.

'Doctor, can I have a word with you? My husband can't bear to go through all the tests and treatments. If he does have a terminal illness, he doesn't want to suffer, go on living. He doesn't want to endure all those endless treatments. We have made living wills. We have agreed to assist each other with suicide... We need two doctors' signatures, do you think you can handle this for me?

'By the way, I would really like to go on holiday. I feel I need it. And I have always dreamt of visiting Ghana, those wonderful medieval castles. I have some cash put aside, enough for two people to have a fantastic time.'

'I'll see what I can do.'

'Thank you, Doctor. I think we understand each other.' She patted him quickly on his hand.

When she got Tony home she put him straight to bed.

'Tony, darling, it's all fine. You won't have to go into hospital, you won't have to undergo any tests or any treatments. The doctor has agreed to my plan.'

'What plan?'

'I mean, how to proceed. I told him about our living wills. He and I will assist you to commit suicide.'

'Did he say it was cancer, then?'

'Yes he did, very aggressive and quite advanced already. Not much hope for you, my poor darling.'

'Oh, I didn't think it was that bad.'

'I'm afraid it is.'

Tony's diarrhoea continued. He got worse and worse. In the end he wanted to die.

'Help me, help me. Pull the plug.'

Elsa called Dr Kalumba.

'Charlie, he's ready.'

Dr Kalumba had managed to get the signature of one of his colleagues under some pretence for a hospital clinical research project. The doctor, who was about to retire, didn't even look at the paper and signed it absent-mindedly.

He arrived at their house late that night.

Tony was unsettled, in pain from taking Senna for such a long time.

'We are ready for you, Mr Radcliffe. I'm going to give you an injection. You won't feel a thing.'

'Thank you, Doctor.'

The last thing Tony remembered was that Elsa had a sneering, rather demonic expression on her face. She smiled and squeezed his hand.

'Goodbye, Tony.'

One month later, Elsa was in a departure lounge at Heathrow Airport about to board a plane to Accra with her compliant, handsome doctor...

Suddenly two plain-clothes policemen appeared behind her.

'Excuse me, are you Mrs Elsa Radcliffe?'

So in my opinion, those in favour should carry a 'Euthanasia' card just as we carry donor cards. If people don't believe in, or don't want to contemplate, euthanasia, they would be exempted. Furthermore, three doctors' signatures would be needed rather than two... And I really like the idea of end-of-life doulas or midwives...

Monkey Brotherly Love

I don't want to fall in love
I don't want to fall out of love
I don't want to marry
I don't want to divorce
I don't want children to love
Who don't love me
I don't want to have a richly paid job
And then lose it
I don't want to be a good boss
Then make my staff redundant
I don't want to know what it is to be rich
Then become poor
I don't want to make friends with those
Who will then despise me.

Why do I write? This book is not quixotic, picaresque, dystopian or utopian, not even a personal odyssey. I extrapolate, get on my imaginary soapbox and note down a few story ideas at the same time. I know it's disjointed. Yet I still have this urge to pour stuff out. I do have a story inside me, my story. Some of it might be a fantasy – fabrications I've composed in my mind. So what? Write it down, whoever I am. Even though I'll never find a publisher.

The farmer in the dressing gown dream

I'm living, poverty-stricken, on an isolated farm on the moors with a wife! We have several domesticated cats and dogs but no livestock. The place is untidy and very dirty. We have a couple of people staying (Damien and Susannah) and my wife is upset at the mess. Deposits of long hairs, cobwebs, dust, flaky skin, discarded earwax, dried bogeys, and shit are everywhere.

This dream seems so real, more so than the squeaky-clean visions I see in the media.

Grosz, the ginger cat, is sleeping on our bed. I kick him off. Damien, Susannah and my wife leave unexpectedly during the night. At dawn I try to clear up and then I decide to go into town for supplies. I get on my motorbike, still in my blue towelling dressing gown. Someone has mentioned two women (prostitutes) are missing. As I steer my bike on the track over the grey barren landscape the headlight catches two decapitated women's heads stuck in the mud. They both have long curly dark hair. They look so natural and at ease, as if they have always been there. They are smiling.

My dark shadowy side. Good and evil in all of us and all that. The efforts of politicians or the clergy haven't improved the human psyche. Many of us are still deprived of education. We haven't learnt to stop being cruel and vicious. I could abuse, violate, kill, but I never have, never will.

Christian martyrs were often sinners first. They fornicated, ate and drank too much and usually came from rich families. Then they repented, shed their former selves, and took up the cloak of poverty. Francis, Augustine? Dominic? Benedict? I have said I could have been a priest…except I don't believe, and other things. I'm not the same person all the time. We all have many selves. Like Tony Perkins in the Hitchcock film, *Psycho*, I dream I am a woman, becoming a female to hide my male sadistic tendencies…

Letter to Daily Mail

We are warmongering imbeciles who never learn from history. We conquer countries, kill the natives, take away their land, rob them of their natural resources and segregate the living. As children, we who are abused become abusers. Post Holocaust, many Jews feel they have a divine right to make war against Palestinians. Nationalistic tendencies and tribalism never cease.

Then the Labour tragedy of Blair, intoxicated by power and war crazy. Brown, bitter and twisted, failed to call an early election, making way for contemptuous Coalition politicians.

Ed Miliband stood against David. No brotherly love there. A sad day for Brit politics.

Or did they mutually agree to this?

The Tories are right, of course. The longest-lasting post war world recession is all the fault of Gordon Brown. Nothing to do with barmy bankers, hedge fund betting, sub-prime lending, stock market frauds or the Euro collapsing.

Prime ministers and Presidents never retain a lasting reputation or respect. Cameron and co. are all who remain.

Lots of jobs for under-educated degenerates like me. No need for benefit. We all have equal abilities.

The privileged rich are no better off than the poor underprivileged. The Tories are right and I am wrong.

Yours

Dorek

PS Bring back hanging!!!

'Religions such as Catholicism are hypocritical,' I said to Mungo. He was never that interested in what I had to say about religion, but I wanted to explain my point of view:

'Historically, popes come from a long line of corrupt politicians; political heads of the Papal States who made their illegitimate children cardinals. Most rural priests were married up until around the tenth century, so why did the Catholic Church start cracking down on them, forcing them to be celibate by the twelfth century?'

'The present pope seems OK, though, better than that German one with his fancy hats and red shoes. Strange he abdicated...'

'If he wasn't gay, I'd eat his hat... What annoys me is that he still dresses like the pope, so are there two popes now?'

'That Benedict looks a bit like you, Dee...'

'What bent dick?'

'Seriously though, I bet loadsa priests aren't celibate.'

'Of course not, it's a contradiction in terms. They must have basic urges, unless they are impotent like me.'

'They aren't allowed sex with women or men, but they still do it.'

'If I'd been a priest I could have coped with the celibacy, but not the hypocrisy.'

'You could have become an Anglican vicar, though. I can just see you...'

'Anglicism is logically weakened by the premise that Henry VIII wanted a divorce. The dissolution of the monasteries, not very Christian, was it?'

'What about all this terrorism then? All these factions, Sunnis and Shias...?

'Islamist extremists give their whole religion a bad name. Strange really, cos IRA militants who condoned terrorism and violence weren't ever considered as Catholic extremists.'

'All that killing and maiming, raping and stoning women makes me want to puke.'

'Judaism's slightly better but too bogged down in historical traditions.'

'Yeah, all that Sabbath stuff, different fridges for foods, no electricity whatever, barmy or what? I admire Buddhism though.'

'Yeah, I like their vegetarianism, but fat Buddha isn't very appealing. I prefer Hinduism. It's colourful and jolly, but there're too many confusing gods. Then of course there's Scientology.'

'Yeah, Clientology, as I call it, is more modern and abstract, but it's all about money,' said Mungo, 'and people are so stupid they give loadsa money to their so-called Church.'

Last time I saw Mungo we talked about Damien, as usual:

'Damien's odd, we all know that. But he's a good guy really. You know that one-legged transvestite tramp? He's been released.'

'What, he's been arrested? What for? I thought Damien and Susannah weren't pressing charges about him.'

'No, they aren't. Damien's letting him live in his garden studio in Suffolk. He's now doing odd jobs for them on a regular basis. Susannah was really against it at first, but even she seems to tolerate him now.'

'Tottenham?'

This next part is another thing I have been avoiding.

Mungo, my best, most beloved friend, died from a brain haemorrhage very unexpectedly. We loved each other very much but in an asexual 'agender' way. Neither of us was interested in sex. That's why we got on so well, like spiritual brothers. Even though we didn't resemble each other physically (like the Elles) and had different tastes in clothes and furniture, we shared the same sense of humour. Still Laurel and Hardy, whatever I thought.

When Mungo went, I experienced physical grief. I felt sick, my heart pounded like a heavy weight in my chest. This was much worse than when Rosa died. Then I was in a daze – it all happened so quickly I was too shocked to feel any physical symptoms. Then I was more in control of my emotions. I never let myself cry, otherwise I would have been called a sissy at school. Now I was older, wiser, my emotions were freer. I was more relaxed about allowing my feelings to hit the surface. I cried like a baby.

Mungo had phlebitis in his thigh. He was prescribed warfarin, which technically is rat poison and thins the blood. Unbeknownst to us all, Mungo had weak capillaries in his brain. The warfarin caused his brain to haemorrhage. He was working at his bench in his Hatton Garden shop, trying to rest his leg on a stool after being told by his GP to keep it horizontal. He complained to Jim, his shop assistant, of having a terrible headache, and then he collapsed. When Jim phoned for the ambulance Mungo was already in a coma. The paramedics drove him immediately to University College hospital. He never woke up. At first, I wasn't allowed to see him as I wasn't a relative. Yolanda had died a couple of years previously so there was no one particularly close to him except for the Elles. In the end I insisted that I saw him. And I was there when they switched off the machines. He looked peaceful, fast asleep, rather than dead. Unlike Rosa. When I'd accompanied her in the ambulance, her hazel eyes had looked vacant, as if her spirit – or her soul – or her essence, whatever, had swiftly left her body. The Elles and I stood round his bed, some praying, others lost in our own thoughts. Like me, Mungo wasn't religious, and though we frequented the Italian club above the church we never attended mass. Yet he would have approved of his funeral being held in the St Paul's Italian Church, which was kindly arranged by the Elles. It was a good send-off in the mock-Rococo surroundings: the electric candles, the lavish white flower arrangements, a soprano singing *Ave Maria*. He's buried in Finchley cemetery and every so often I visit his grave, change the plants. Luella, Luanna and Loretta still go too.

I have never understood why he made me his sole heir. Childlessness in Mungo's family was epidemic, no I meant endemic, and I never ever discovered any other possible relatives, except the Elles who seemed sincerely pleased by my surprise inheritance. Mungo's estate included what he had been left by Yolanda. They had shared various investments, and a property portfolio, and they even owned a block of flats in Islington, but when she had died Mungo had divested most of it and ended up with a great load of cash.

After the funeral expenses, which were covered by his bank (his solicitor arranged this), I paid for the headstone that we erected almost a year later. I wanted a plain one but I knew he would have wanted something fancy, so it has two Rococo angels surrounding an obelisk with geometric designs, inscribed:

Gerardo 'Mungo' Danielov 1949 – 2009

When I received the cheque from his solicitor about nine months after he died, I couldn't bear to tell people that it was in seven figures. I had no idea what to do with all the money. I had no nieces and nephews, so I distributed cheques to my cousins' children. I must admit some weren't at all grateful. I got official acknowledgements, but not exactly a thank you, from four of them, via their parents. A couple of them never even responded. I also donated to various charities: The National Anti-Vivisection Society, RSPB, National Trust, 38 Degrees, Greenpeace, Friends of the Earth, St Barnardo's, NSPCC, Amnesty International, even the Labour Party, and of course the Otosclerosis Society.

I worried about how I was going to cope with my deafness without Mungo's help. I started carrying a card in my wallet saying I have a hearing loss:

'Please face me, speak clearly, don't shout, write your message if necessary.'

If I couldn't hear, I learnt to ask people, such as when I couldn't hear train or tube announcements. And I learnt to say 'I suffer from severe hearing impairment' rather than 'I'm deaf' as usually many people responded by saying: 'So am I!'

When Mungo left me his family house in Holloway, I wasn't sure what to do with it. Clerkenwell was undergoing great changes, and after Yolanda died, the building where she'd had her shop and upstairs flat was in a prime property area and very sought after. From what I could gather, she had leased the building from the council, via a charitable trust, and when I moved in I was treated in the same way as a controlled tenant. So they couldn't shift me, even after she died, it transpired. This made me feel guilty. After a few months of indecision, I moved to Holloway. It was an ideal opportunity for Islington Council to sell the valuable property while I moved into the larger Victorian house.

I've always liked the idea of living in a sparse, minimalist environment, but it was surprising how quickly the rooms filled with all my books. I had got rid of some of my old stuff in Leather Lane and most of Mungo's possessions as well, which I mainly donated to Islington charity shops. Walter and Dino helped me arrange the removal of everything after I had asked a few people, including them, the Elles and Jim, Mungo's assistant, what they wanted of Mungo's.

Damien said he didn't want anything. I came to an agreement with Jim that he could take over Mungo's workshop. Basically I gave him the business for free.

I bought a few pieces of modern furniture, including a new bed and wardrobe. Walter came to help me with the delivery of my new king-size bed.

'The delivery van is here!'

I thought he said 'hanger on', which is nothing like delivery van! I had visions of people knocking on my door asking for money.

I was discovering paintings and antiques. I became a collector of modern art and quirky furniture, ornaments and whatever else took my fancy. Art Deco, fifties' stuff, but Georgian occasional tables and a wonderful mahogany desk where I am writing now.

I became a volunteer for the Otosclerosis Society. It secmcd fitting. The more books I read, the more I realised how many people were deaf. David Lodge, Julian Barnes, that actress Stephanie Beacham, and of course the amazing percussionist Dame Evelyn Glennie. She has a perfect sense of rhythm, unlike me. Even Princess Alice, the mother of Prince Philip, was stone deaf. She lip-read like me, but she had strange medical treatments and visited Freud. Otosclerosis can be hormone-related, so her reproductive organs were X-rayed. She was institutionalised and abandoned by her husband, Prince Andrew of Greece.

So I'm a deaf, unmarried childless person who has inherited loadsa money. No one will feel sorry for me. I don't want them to, but it's funny how things turned out…

I have also inherited Mungo's dog, Bingo. After all these years, I finally have the pet I always wanted. He's a great help, almost like a hearing-dog because he listens out for me: he barks if someone is coming up the doorstep before they even have time to ring the bell. He also barks at the telephones. I had special loud bells suited to my hearing frequencies fitted to both extensions. When they both ring I can hear a hilarious cacophony of barking dog and tenor trillings in unison. Quite often I don't answer the phone and the call is automatically switched to the answer machine with a message from me saying: 'Please send me a text instead.'

I've got a kitten too, from Holloway's cat refuge. I love cats. I was always nagging Rosa to get me a kitten but she wouldn't budge. She wouldn't even get me a budgie. Said I wouldn't remember to feed it, and having a cat as a pet, well, it just wouldn't be fair in a small flat like hours, I mean ours. But now I have a garden, the dog and the cat can run around. She's grey and white and I've called her Rosie. And Bingo seems to have accepted her pretty quickly. They lie in his basket together and eat from the same dishes. Bingo can't believe his luck as he now gets cat food to eat as well as his own. Bingo is a Yorkshire terrier and doesn't need much exercise, but I take him for long walks. I do the walking and carry him most of the way when we are climbing upwards. Hampstead Heath is our favourite, and as it's not that far from Holloway we walk from the house. It's like a different world up there. I love the heath, the pond, the green expanse, the wind in my hair.

Living on my own for so many years, I often talk to myself. Not that surprising really – many people do... I make out I am talking to Bingo:

> *Good is god, god is good, dog is good,*
> *Food is good, fog is not.*
> *Bad is dad, dad is dead, never knew my dad,*
> *Neither of them.*
> *Dem dere shoes are dead, don't wear them den*
> *Nice weather outside,*
> *So go for a walk,*
> *Shall I wear de canvas or de rubber?*

What day is today?
Monday man goes for de walk
Tuesday de shoes need repairing
Or do I buy new ones?
Wensday walkies in de new shoes
Firsday for walking de bingo
Friday free to do nuffink
Satday sitting for de reading and de writing.
Sunday sunshine, sunning meself at de pond.

Bingo misses Mungo as much as I do. I tell him what Mungo said to me once:

'Now, take it easy.'

'Down? I'm not your dog.'

I do say 'Down, boy' a lot to Bingo when he gets too affectionate and starts licking my face, and it's true what they say about dogs and their owners. I can see a resemblance between Bingo and Mungo.

Mungo, my dear Mungo. I will always think of you as my monkey, our monkey brotherly love…

Julia in Prague

The dichotomy of loving
Why do we fall in love
With people we should
Instinctively hate?
Twittering like a budgie,
Chatting to them online
On Facebook or scrutinising
Them on Skype like a hawk.
Searching for them maniacally
In every new text message
Or email we see,
When we know worshipping
That particular person
Is absolute madness.
Their admirable qualities
Outweighed by their
Vile cruelty
And weak sense of humour.
We are emotional weathercocks
Blind to their faults.
Later with the realisation
That our love has turned
To hate, we chameleon-change.
With hair-tearing despair we
Despise our former lovers,
Like a wind turbine out of control.
Hatred rumbles
In our guts.
Now we can't even

Abide their names,
Let alone look them up
On the Internet.

This chapter was written after my trip to Prague, Budapest and Warsaw. Warsaw I found very disappointing. Buda and Pest were my favourite places, but this story is influenced by the impressions I gained of Prague. I finished it in my new creative writing evening class in London Cosmo College.

(Rosa said it was typical to over-estimate doctors when they act like gods.)

Julia came to Prague to be with Juraj. He was a novelist and they had met in London at an author acquaintance's reading in the Hampstead Waterstones. In spite of her unromantic nature, Julia felt an instant pull and attraction to him, and it had been mutual. Juraj looked the typical intellectual, tall but stooping, with balding brown curly hair and full beard, craggy face, and round rimless glasses. She thought that he resembled Umberto Eco. Julia was above average height and angular, with long ash-blonde hair and large amber green eyes. She had never married although she had been in a few long-term relationships with men, without feeling committed to any of them. With Juraj she felt different, as if this was the first time she had fallen in love.

She was a writer, but made her living by proofreading and part-time journalism. When she met Juraj he extended his visit to London and stayed with her, but then had to get back to Prague. And after a couple of years of enduring a long-distance relationship with hurried trips by him to London or her to the Czech Republic, she decided to rent out her North London flat and move to Prague to be with Juraj on a more or less permanent basis. A change of scene might give her some creative impetus and improve her writing. They were both in their early fifties so it wasn't young love; they were more like best friends than passionate lovers. It was companionship they both craved. Juraj was widowed. He was lonely and missed having a woman around. He had wanted to marry Julia quite soon after they met, but Julia had had reservations. She had always been wary of giving all of herself to another person, but she was gradually coming round to the idea. Juraj was trying to persuade her that they should get married in Prague. Tackling Czech bureaucracy as a married couple rather than living together would be much easier. She was still hesitating. She wanted to settle down first, taste the city – and the people.

Juraj was quite well known as an author, and was making a relatively comfortable living, writing contemporary novels about life in Eastern Europe after the collapse of the Iron Curtain. He had always been politically involved, especially in the struggle against censorship, and had endured great hardship as a young writer under the Communist regime. He was enjoying his new-found wealth and was happy to support Julia, but she was determined to keep her financial independence. Julia didn't earn as much from her writing as Juraj. She'd had a few short stories published in magazines and was attempting to write a novel, but most of her meagre income came from proofreading, which she continued to do via email. With the move to Prague she had missed a few new jobs and was now only working for the one publisher. Although she was getting regular income from the rent on her flat it wasn't enough to cover any luxury items. Juraj suggested she could teach English and said he would make enquiries. Julia wasn't sure – she wasn't a qualified teacher, but Juraj assured her that this wasn't important. The Czech people he knew needed help with English conversation and she would be ideal.

In the meantime, Julia was desperately trying to learn Czech and enrolled in an evening class, held every Friday. On the very first evening, she started talking to an interesting looking man who, like her, was having trouble coping with the indigenous language. He had worked in England for several years, but had recently been offered a job at the University Hospital in Prague as a consultant paediatrician. He was very chatty and warm, and told her his mother was English and his father was Indian. They had moved to England from Bombay before he was born. Julia thought he, Keki Patloo, was extremely attractive – resembling a slimmer and more youthful Placido Domingo. He must have been in his forties, and as Julia looked younger than her years they could have been mistaken for being a similar age. They exchanged views about life in Prague and their various experiences. Keki missed London, but as he told Julia:

'Prague is lovely, quite compact and very Parisian in nature. Very different to the enormous metropolitan mass of London where I used to work. I love walking around, when I have time, that is.'

Julia agreed:

'I love walking from the Charles Bridge into the old centre, watching the boats on the Vitava River as I go. And all the magnificent gothic and baroque buildings, like the Prasna Brana, and I love the art deco building next to it as well: the Obecni Dun is a wonderful place. I really enjoy the concerts; I've seen both the Prague Symphony and the Czech Philharmonic there. But I haven't ventured anywhere outside the centre yet.'

'The outskirts are quite dismal, you know, and there is a tremendous amount of poverty. In London it was never so obvious, and, actually, I'm afraid you do get accustomed to seeing people sleeping rough in the streets there. Not as bad as Bombay, though. Here it's different, not the individuals on the streets, but whole tenements full of exceedingly poor families living hand to mouth.'

'I feel guilty about all this poverty, both here and in London,' replied Julia. 'Sometimes I wonder if they were really worse off under the communist regime, but Vaclav Havel has been such an inspirational leader, you can't fault him. I'm sure they're trying very hard to eradicate poverty. I know these things take time, but I'm constantly thinking I would like to help somehow.'

'Well, there're lots of things to do at the hospital. If you felt like being a volunteer, we need all the help we can get.' He smiled and gave her a penetrating stare.

Julia took a deep breath:

'Okay, yes, why not? What would I have to do?'

Keki put his arm round her. Julia was surprised by this action, but felt very relaxed with him. 'I'll introduce you to Marta. She'll interview you and tell you how you can help us. Come to the hospital next Monday morning. But please drop into my office first, on the fifth floor.'

When Julia got home that night she mentioned to Juraj that she had met Keki who had suggested she could do some voluntary work at the local hospital. She didn't mention that he was very handsome. Julia was menopausal. Her hormones were jumping around, making her more aware of sexual arousal. Even though she had read that many women lose interest in sex at this time, the opposite had happened to her. Juraj had entered her life at an apposite moment.

'I know I won't get paid, but I want to do something worthwhile.'

'Good for you. It might lead to some English teaching as well.'

Juraj was always so encouraging. He teased her but never criticised her; sometimes she wished he would. In the five or so years they had known each other they had never argued.

Juraj never lost his temper, never shouted at her. He seemed perennially tranquil. He was lucky to have such inner peace, considering the hard life he had led in Prague, she thought. When he had lived with her in London briefly, it had given him a breathing space, a time for reflection and positive thought. When they had met he had felt so alone, so alien in a big cosmopolitan city like London. Only after one month or so of meeting him, Julia had invited him to stay at her flat. He had been so grateful; she had given him the grounding he desperately needed. A good woman to love and cherish *and* a comfortable home to live in. He had felt so fortunate. She was his lucky mascot and he still felt that way about her. During his sojourn in London, he had become very energetic and creative. The words just flowed out of him. Julia had been so supportive, and when more recently he had suggested she move to Prague, he hadn't been able to believe it when she'd said yes – that she would give up everything in London to be with him. Julia had not found it too difficult to agree to the move. On the contrary: her parents were both dead and her two sisters lived abroad, one in New York and one in Melbourne, so she had no real ties in London. Obviously she would miss her friends, but many of them would relish visiting her in Prague.

Juraj still thought of his beloved first wife, but he was very content with Julia. She wasn't at all demanding like other women (except when it came to sex). She had a strong character and an independent spirit that he found amazing – and he loved her sense of humour – she called him Frank after Franz Kafka.

'Frank; the importance of being Frank. You're so frank, Frank.'

He was as head-over-heels in love with her as when they had first met. Sometimes he was unsure if she felt the same way about him – perhaps she wasn't as crazy about him as he was about her. She always held a part of herself back, but she seemed happy enough and she looked more beautiful than ever, positively glowing.

On Monday morning Julia got the bus to the hospital, and found the fifth floor office of Professor Keki Patloo after a few wrong turns. He was on the phone when she entered the room. She stood at the door waiting for him to finish his call. When he did, he got up, came up to her and kissed her on both cheeks.

'Julia, it's lovely to see you. You look stunning.'

Julia felt embarrassed. It was true she had made some effort and put on some smart clothes and more make-up than usual. He was being over-effusive but she enjoyed it exceedingly, and the way he lingeringly kissed her cheeks.

(Another creative writing rule: never use adverbs, but I like them!)

Although they had only met once, his affection seemed perfectly natural. They chatted about general things, and it turned out they even shared some mutual acquaintances in London. Julia had once covered a medical conference on breast cancer for a magazine and had made friends with two colleagues of Keki from St Thomas's hospital. He then showed her some of the books he had written, mainly about paediatric care for the long-term sick, with the emphasis on how essential it was to make children feel comfortable and hospitals child-friendly environments. One book was mainly about hospital architecture, interior decoration and furniture, which she found very interesting. She had never liked the idea of those gloomy Victorian edifices, and thought modern well-designed hospitals so much better.

Keki possessed the typically good doctor's bedside manner of making people feel comfortable, as if he had known them for years. Julia loved looking at him – he was a very finely made man, graceful, tall, slim, with smooth golden skin and a little mole high on his right cheek.

He introduced her to Marta, one of the chief nursing officers who looked quite young considering her senior position. She was dark-haired and petite with all the curves in the right places and very flirtatious with the handsome doctor, even fluttering her eyelashes at him, which seemed ludicrous behaviour to Julia.

Marta ushered Julia out of Keki's office down to her own on the fourth floor. Julia was reluctant to leave Keki; there were so many things she wanted to discuss with him, and it was good to speak in English to someone other than Juraj. Marta explained that there was a rota for volunteers: morning, afternoon or evening. Marta asked Julia in Czech what work she did and Julia explained, haltingly, that she was a writer. The main problem was obviously her lack of the language, but working in a Czech hospital would be an ideal way of learning it. Marta decided that first off Julia would be of most help in the administrative office where she could help with menial tasks such as photocopying and filing, but that eventually when her Czech improved she could possibly help out in the library, and even read to some of the children in the paediatrics ward. Julia was delighted with this suggestion and was determined to improve her Czech as quickly as possible. She was already thinking of a story she could write about the children's ward.

She arranged with Marta to go in three consecutive afternoons a week, starting Tuesday. Before she left the hospital, she decided to say goodbye to Keki, but when she reached his office on the fifth floor, he wasn't there. She felt very disappointed but hoped to see him at her Czech class on Friday.

When Julia arrived at the class, slightly late, she was

even more disappointed to see that Keki wasn't already there, and he didn't turn up at all that evening.

The following day, after a morning spent working on her novel, she went to the hospital and one of the admin clerks showed her the work she was expected to do. She soon got the hang of it, as she always did, and found that working on the files with the Czech alphabet was really useful. After her shift had finished, she decided once again to go up and find Keki on the fifth floor. This time he was sitting at his desk. She poked her head around the door and he greeted her with a great big smile.

'Julia, come in, how lovely to see you.' He kissed her on both cheeks and gave her a long hug as well.'

'I missed you at the class last Friday.'

'Oh, I don't suppose I'll make it every week. I'm just so busy here. I have bought some tapes; hopefully I can catch up with my Czech that way. By the way, did you say you were looking for English students? One of my colleagues, Dr Artur, is interested. I'll introduce you to him. Hey, look, I'm almost finished here for now – I have to come back later on tonight, but I could do with a break. Why don't I get him now, and we can all go for a drink together?' He gave her one of his intent looks, as if to say how could she refuse?

She didn't want to refuse, and said, 'Yes, why not?'

So Keki, Dr Artur and Julia ended up going to a divine art-deco bar and drinking quantities of Czech beer. Dr Armin Artur, a fellow consultant paediatrician, was an old-world gentleman with coiffured white hair and pointed beard, aquiline distinguished features; the type of man Julia seldom met in London. His English was reasonably good:

'I would very much like help with conversation. I write English very better than speak it. The pronunciation, the idiomatic expressions, they are very puzzling to me.'

Julia was delighted; in a space of a week she had

voluntary work at the hospital and also her first pupil! They arranged to meet at the hospital after her Wednesday shift and she would give him lessons there. Keki was being very attentive and buying all the drinks. He was such a generous, outgoing person, and quite unlike anyone she had ever met before. He was outlandish yet down to earth, but then again he was a doctor; doctors could be crude. He was telling silly jokes and trying to explain English innuendo to Dr Artur.

'Oh, Vicar, what's that in your pocket, or are you just pleased to see me? That, Armin, means he had an erection.'

They were laughing like mad people; Julia hadn't enjoyed herself so much in ages. Although she was growing used to life in Prague, the language was still proving difficult and this was making it hard for her to make friends. When they left Dr Artur shook her hand, but Keki and Julia gave each other a long hug and kissed each other three times on the cheek.

Julia felt peculiar. She was sexually attracted to Keki. She loved that mole on his cheek.

'How stupid of me!' She knew she was behaving like a foolish teenager. She had always had such a cool attitude to men. Yet after Juraj, she had become more attuned to sexual responses. She had to get back to Juraj – start to feel normal again. But she couldn't stop thinking about Keki. As she and Juraj were preparing their evening meal together, she described her work at the hospital and the drink afterwards, but instead of being excited about giving English lessons to Dr Artur, she felt more elated about having spent time with Keki.

Unusually for her, Julia got into a routine: three afternoons at the hospital and a Wednesday evening slot for English lessons with Dr Artur. Afterwards they often went for a quick drink and carried on speaking in English, and Keki joined them occasionally. He seemed to have given up completely on the Czech evening class so Julia looked forward to seeing him at the bar instead. She was always downcast when he didn't show up. She caught glances of him at the hospital but he was always rushing around. Sometimes he looked absolutely exhausted and her heart went out to him. Coping with very sick or dying children was stressful. She wished she could help him somehow.

One Saturday morning, Julia was queuing up at the baker's for some bread. The queues were usually tediously long. In front of her was a very attractive blonde woman, not unlike Meryl Streep, Julia thought. According to Juraj, this was Julia's most annoying habit – comparing people she met with celebrities. Juraj thought this part of her Americanised western culture, no doubt. Holding the hand of the woman was a young boy. Julia realised he was speaking in English. She had never seen such a beautiful child. Unlike his very fair-skinned mother (Julia presumed she was his mother) he had a dark olive complexion with blue black hair and green eyes, and the longest, curliest eyelashes she had ever seen nestling on his cheeks.

Julia had never been maternal, but this child was so beautiful, she couldn't help saying something to him:

'Oh, you speak English.'

'Yes, of course I do. I was born in England.'

His mother ruffled his head and said in Czech: 'Now be nice to the lady, Tomas.'

'And how old are you?' asked Julia.

'I am six years, four months and ten days.'

Julia laughed.

'How precise of you.'

The woman also laughed. 'He's very interested in mathematics,' she said with a surprisingly good English accent.

'Are you English?' Julia asked her.

'No I am Czech, but I lived in England for several years.

I married a doctor there, but we have come back to live in Prague, where I grew up.'

'I have moved to Prague recently myself.'

They exchanged a few more facts about each other and then introduced themselves. The Meryl Streep look-alike was called Hana.

Julia mentioned Juraj's name.

'Oh yes, Juraj Becher. I've tried to get my husband to read one of his novels, but Keki says his Czech isn't that good yet.'

'Keki?' asked Julia. 'You mean Keki Patloo?' Keki had never even mentioned a wife or a son.

'Yes, why? Do you know him?'

'Why yes. I met him at an evening class but he doesn't come any more.'

'Oh, that's odd, I thought he was still going,' said Hana, frowning her impeccably smooth, high forehead.

'Well' Julia swallowed heavily 'I still do see him occasionally at the hospital where I'm doing some voluntary work. And I'm giving English lessons to Dr Artur.'

'Oh, Armin Artur, he's such a delightful man!'

'Yes, he is.' Although Julia wasn't keen on the way Dr Artur now simultaneously kissed her hand and clicked his heels.

Tomas started tugging at his mother's sleeve. It was her turn to be served.

'Well, it was lovely meeting you. Look, if you ever fancy coffee sometime, Julia, I normally have a late breakfast at Petr's Café in the Stare Mesto – the Old Town – after I've dropped Tomas off at school.'

'Yes, I know it. That would be great, Hana. Maybe next Friday?'

So the two women started to meet up, usually on a Friday when Julia wasn't quite so busy. Julia wanted women friends and thought Hana her type of person. Although they discussed their respective men, Julia was careful not to say anything too much about Keki. 'Oh by the way, Hana, I find your husband extremely attractive!' was something she preferred to keep to herself.

Hana had explained how she and Keki met. After studying English at Charles University, Hana had been very lucky to get a visa for England through her aunt in Newcastle. After a few weeks staying at her aunt's, she had moved to London, working as a waitress, and at a rock concert –Talking Heads were playing – she had literally bumped into her future husband.

'I fell in love with Keki gradually. It definitely wasn't love at first sight. He was very different to anyone I'd ever met, both physically and intellectually, partly because he was nine years older. I thought the fact that he was half-Indian might be a problem for my family in Prague, but happily I was mistaken.

'When my parents came to visit me in London, they both fell for Keki – for them it was love at first sight! We decided to get married there and then, while my parents were visiting.'

Hana's paperwork had taken some sorting out, but they managed it. Keki's father, who was a Parsee, and his mother were uncharacteristically relaxed about the sudden registry office wedding and hit it off very well with Hana's parents at the reception at Kettner's in Soho. Keki had just joined St Thomas's Hospital as one of the youngest consultant paediatricians ever appointed there. They bought a house in Camberwell, and Tomas had been born a year later. Hana gave up waitressing, and any hope of finding a more interesting job, to look after the baby, and spent her free time decorating the house.

Now in Prague, Hana still hadn't found any work, but she was working on her Master's degree in Philosophy, which she was doing part-time, and attending a course in Renaissance art history once a week at the Charles University while Tomas was at school.

On the fourth occasion they met, Julia walked into the café and found Hana looking terrible. She had no make-up on and her eyes were red and puffy.

'Hana, what's wrong?' Hana put her head in her hands and mumbled: 'It's… it's Keki, he's been having an affair!'

'What?' Julia blushed. Nothing was going on between her and Keki, but she had thought about it. When they were alone together, there was definitely a sexual charge between them. Once or twice he had stroked her hair. Even though she was older than him, she knew he found her attractive.

'Who' she swallowed heavily 'who with?'

Julia felt personally affronted, as if he had been unfaithful to her too.

'With Marta, the senior nursing officer.'

'Oh no! God, she's so obvious, how could he be tempted by her?'

Hana looked up at Julia. She seemed to be taking this very personally.

'How sweet of you to care so much…' Hana said. 'Well, you know you told me he hadn't been attending the Czech evening class? He kept telling me he was. I was suspicious and went through his clothes one night. There were some… some… Durex in his pocket' she sobbed 'and two tickets to the cinema. For *Robocop III*, the kind of movie he would never go to see. He used to laugh at the thought of people actually paying good money to see rubbish like that.

'But how do you know it's M- M- Marta?' stammered Julia.

'I confronted him and he confessed. He said she was always trying it on with him, and in the end he just relented. And he's promised to stop seeing her, but I don't know if I can believe him. He works really closely with that… that woman. Julia, you have to help me. I have to put a stop to this, and teach *her* a lesson.

'What can I do, Hana? It's nothing to do with me.'

'You'll think of something. How shall I say, you can be more subversive than me. Please help me. I thought about ripping up Keki's clothes, doing something to hurt him. But it's her, the bitch, it's her I want to hurt. Why can't she leave married men alone? There must be millions of men out there she could have chosen.'

Julia couldn't reply. Her mind was racing. It was true that Marta was a terrible flirt, but why did Keki succumb? Julia was livid with him, and actually, if she was honest with herself, jealous. She pulled herself together.

'Hana, look, don't do anything stupid. I'll help you. I'll try to think of something. I see Marta every time I go to the hospital. I'll keep an eye on her.'

'Oh, Julia, thank you. I'm really trying to forgive Keki for what he's done. It's going to be very difficult, I know, but I must try, for Tomas's sake most of all. Keki says it's never happened before, and it will never happen again. But I just don't trust that Marta. She's there every day at the hospital with him, throwing herself at him. I do rather understand why he was tempted.'

Julia didn't agree with the saintly Hana. There was such a thing as self-control, but she didn't say anything. Well, this was a turn up for the books. All the time she had thought she and Keki were having a mild flirtation, he was having sex with Marta.

Julia was helping out in the library now. Her Czech had improved enormously, and she was reading to the young patients. The next time she was at the hospital she took the lift straight up to Marta's room. Julia greeted Marta as she did normally. Julia couldn't help but like her. She was always so cheerful and jolly, and actually very competent at her job. Julia didn't know what to say; she couldn't find any appropriate words. She made an excuse about borrowing some Sellotape and went back down to the library.

What could they do to teach Marta a lesson? Write her an anonymous letter, the kind where you cut out individual letters from magazine or newspaper headings?

'PLEASE LEAVE DR PATLOO ALONE. IF YOU DON'T, YOUR LIFE WILL BE IN DANGER.'

Oh, that was just too silly. What else could they say?

'YOU BITCH, FUCK OFF AND LEAVE THE DOCTOR ALONE.'

It was all so juvenile. She couldn't possibly write such rubbish. She could try again to have a quiet word with Marta, but she knew it wouldn't do any good. Marta would say it was none of her business, which it wasn't. Maybe there were alternative ways of teaching someone a lesson. This situation reminded Julia of the apocryphal story about the husband who had left his wife to set up house with his new lover. The wife went round to their new house while they were both out and stuffed frozen prawns into all the hollow brass curtain rods. The smell became so unbearable that floors were dug up, walls were demolished, and as they still had no idea what was causing it, the puzzled couple eventually moved out, taking the brass curtain rods with them!

Or the one where the wife went round to the lover's house, dialled an Australian number and then left the phone off the hook.

'Oh, it's all so stupid,' she said to herself. She couldn't do anything so pathetic. And what would Keki think of Julia if he found out that she had been involved in these schemes?

The more she thought about it, the only person she could talk to was Keki himself. She was curious to say the least. She needed to talk to him. It would be difficult to find the right moment; he was always so busy. She decided the only way was to get it over with and confront him immediately. She walked towards the lift on the ground floor, and who should be there but Keki himself.

'Keki, I was just coming up to see you.'

'Why Julia, what a lovely surprise. Do get in.'

Keki put his arm round her and they got in the lift together. The lift seemed to take an inordinate amount of time; it was only five floors, for God's sake. Keki was staring at Julia. She felt embarrassed when he looked at her like that. She could have cut the sexual tension with a knife. She started to grin at him, and then realised she was supposed to be angry with him. At that moment the lift stopped, thank goodness. They walked towards his office.

'Keki, I need to speak to you confidentially.'

'Oh yes? What is it you want?' he asked, half-closing his eyes.

'Do you mind if I close the door?'

'Julia, my darling, are you here to make mad, passionate love with me?' he joked.

'Keki, I'm trying to be serious.' She swallowed. On any other day, she would have answered back 'Yes!' but things were different now. 'You know I see Hana, don't you?'

'Yes, she told me you'd become friends.'

'You never mention her. I didn't even know you were married until I met her.'

'Oh, Julia!' He sounded exasperated.

'Look, I don't know how to say this, but Hana has confided in me. It's all rather embarrassing. She's told me about your affair with Marta. She wanted me to warn Marta off somehow, but it's so juvenile. And it's nothing to do with me really.'

Julia paused; she was running out of breath.

'And... I must admit I have feelings for you, though

obviously Hana doesn't know this. I feel such a fool, but I decided I should confront you. Oh Keki, I think I idealised you. I thought you were such a wonderful person and an excellent doctor. Now I discover you're just a cheap adulterer.'

'Oh Julia, please! Don't get sanctimonious on me. Look, I'm a normal heterosexual man – nurses and doctors make passes at each other all the time. Marta and I are just good friends. I have no feelings for her – we have a little bit of sex now and then. I like her, she's fun! You know I like to touch women. I like touching you too, and I'm pleased you have feelings for me.' He laughed.

Julia quickly changed the subject.

'But Hana thinks it's all over between you and Marta. She's trying to forgive you.'

'Look, I love my wife very much. I would do anything for her. I'd rather die than hurt her. In the past whenever I've *played away*, I've always managed to hide it from her and she's never been hurt. Okay, this time she found out, and when she asked me straight out whether I was having an affair, I don't know why, but I confessed. I found that I couldn't lie about it. Anyway, I've already told Marta to lie low for a while.'

'But Keki, you have to end it completely.'

'Okay I will, I will. I promise.'

'It's not me you have to promise, it's for Hana. Keki, I'm so disappointed in you. I thought you were different. Now I discover you're just like any other man, no self-control and no restraint when it comes to sex.'

'Oh Julia, I'm sorry I'm *such* a disappointment to you, but I'm human. I work jolly hard, and sometimes I need some escape.'

'But you're happily married. Why isn't that enough for you?'

'It just isn't – I need other women, lots of them. I always have but Hana will always come first.'

Julia grappled with this fact.

'Well, I feel sorry for you – like a little boy in a sweet shop, not being able to stop eating sweets. That's what sex is for you, and I thought I was being juvenile when I thought about writing Marta one of those stuck-down newsprint anonymous letters.'

Keki laughed. 'You weren't, were you?'

'I thought about it.' Julia laughed as well. Trust Keki to see the funny side. He never seemed to get upset about anything.

'Oh well, I suppose I should get back to my library.'

Keki hugged her.

'I hope we can still be friends. And I promise, I won't see Marta in private ever again.'

'Keki, you need to say that to your wife, not me.'

'I want to be in your good books, Julia. Your good opinion of me matters, seriously. You're intelligent, attractive. I enjoy our talks together. I want us to be friends.'

'Well, we're both too busy for that,' said Julia hurriedly. 'But look, let's just forget we've had this conversation. If you and Marta stop this now, for Hana's sake and for your son's, we'll leave it at that.'

'Okay, Julia, I promise, and I do hope our friendship won't be affected by this, eh, little mishap?' He put his hand on her shoulder.

'We'll see, Dr Patloo, we'll see,' Julia said.

She left the room as fast as she could. He really was incorrigible. He was still flirting with her, and to make matters worse, she was still enjoying it. Hopefully they could be friends; their flirtation had been just a joke, really, she tried convincing herself. It was poor Hana that Keki had really hurt, not her.

Back in the library, Julia was stacking shelves and thinking about what she would tell Hana. She knew Keki really loved Hana. He was just very good at making excuses for himself. He employed the usual male conceit of compartmentalising his life, à la Bill Clinton. Julia was so relieved that nothing had happened between the two of them. For the sake of both Hana and Juraj she was determined to keep it that way.

Julia met Hana for coffee the following Friday.

'Look, Hana, I've seen Marta, and I'm sure everything will be okay. You don't have to worry about her.'

'Oh Julia, I'm so grateful.'

'Maybe you should be worried about me instead,' thought Julia to herself. She pushed these thoughts out of her head. Keki was definitely a no-go area.

She and Juraj had started to make wedding plans. Juraj had been delighted when Julia had agreed that they should get married sooner rather than later. She had also mentioned Keki's affair and had admitted to Juraj that she herself had grown fond of him.

'I know you would never think about other women, but I did find him attractive.'

Juraj, who was very perceptive, might even have guessed that she had wanted to become more deeply involved with Keki. He was, however, the type of man who wouldn't want to hear any grisly details. All he said was:

'I love you very much, Julia, but I'm not as flawless as you think. When I was married to my first wife, I had other women. I can't explain it. I was very much in love with my wife, but I was young. I wanted to taste as much of life as I could. But now, I just want you – I want to live with you until we're very old and very grey – for the rest of my life. It's a simple want, but it's all I want.'

Julia kissed him, saying: 'So you are human after all, my darling! I'll have to take you down from that pedestal!'

She kissed him on the lips, thinking, 'I must marry Juraj now and forget this past silliness. And I do love him, more than I thought.' She knew that she had never loved Keki. He was a very good-looking and entertaining man, but it had been pure sexual attraction. Keki could keep to the Martas of this world.

Hana was delighted when Julia told her the news about the impending marriage.

'Oh, I'm so pleased for you both.'

'You and Keki are both invited to the wedding.'

'Thank you, Julia. You've been a good friend and I know Keki's very fond of you. Things are fine between us now. We still really do love each other, you know.'

Julia hoped that Hana wouldn't go into too much detail. If she was really honest with herself, she still had the occasional yearning for Keki. She tried to speak neutrally.

'I realise how much I love Juraj. When you really love someone, it's more than merely physical – I mean – it's not just about sex. You don't care what your beloved looks like physically. You see his soul instead.'

'Well, Keki's soul is not as unblemished as I thought, but I love him anyway. We wouldn't love them if they were perfect – it would just be too boring.'

They laughed.

The Wonders of Oz

In a nameless middle-eastern country
In working holiday group,
Human rights watching or
Some sort of trade delegation.
Political atmosphere edgy, unsafe
And caught up in some crisis.
Interrogated, tortured and raped.
Faeces stuck up my anus.
Guards lie, saying I shat myself.
It was rapist using his own shit.
I think I am dying, or dead.
Killed by them.
But dream twists. I take control.
Make my escape.
Badly beaten and bruised,
Lips swollen and bleeding,
I wear burka to disguise myself
And join long line of women and children
Leaving building, going through
Endless corridors and stairs,
Finally on to street,
I wake up thinking I'm dead,
But knowing that
I stopped it happening.

The reaction to my Prague story was very disheartening. It didn't get a positive response from either my new teacher, Hannah Friedland, or my fellow creative writers. I'd worked so hard on it, tried to imagine women characters and their relationships to men but it obviously hadn't rung true. So I stopped going to the class and concentrated on planning my trip to Australia and New Zealand instead.

I gave up Lincoln's Inn (rather reluctantly), but hopefully at least some other 'shirker' would enjoy it as much as I had. It was the longest I had ever stayed in a job. I don't even know how many years; must have been at least twenty by now, but I couldn't wait to start my trip.

Uncle Franco's son, also called Franco (why do they do this?), lived in Melbourne, so I arranged to visit him.

Cousin Franco (or Frank as his Oz mates called him), his second, or even third, wife, Adele, who was Australian, and their two young daughters picked me up from the airport in their people carrier and took me to their home in the suburb of Sandringham. They had a modern white weather-boarded house, colonial in style with a wrought-iron balcony overlooking the ocean.

Frank told me about the reason Australia was full of wrought-iron balconies, but I thought he said wartime!

'When raw materials were exported from Oz, the empty ships were filled with pig iron to use as ballast on the return journey to stabilise them, and that's why you see so many wrought-iron balconies on these colonial-style houses.'

The house was mainly on one level with several spacious rooms. Their two young daughters, Zara and Zelda, seemed very intrigued by me and were constantly asking me to play with them. Frank had already explained to me that the money I had sent them was now in a trust fund and he had told them of my generosity. After that it was never mentioned again.

My experience of children was non-existent.

I'm not anti-children: I like them, but I don't want to be force-

fed them. Being a parent is a very important and responsible role, and most people do a good job. Some obviously don't, but I have no desire to berate them. On the other hand, people like me who don't have children, for whatever reason, should not be treated with disdain, or, even worse, pity. Having children is not the 'mother' of all experiences, the 'be all' of existence, and I find it irritating when people say they would feel incomplete if they were childless. Some of us don't need children to have fulfilling lives. I know I am no great example. I have dallied with life, been aimless, haven't gained any sense of achievement, but many childless people are energetic, creative, resolute and successful. And we don't need endless social-media images of the little cherubs doing amazing things at an extremely young age constantly shoved down our throats. Perhaps babies would prefer to be kept out of the Internet limelight.

'Hey Mum, Dad, stop taking photos of me! Take a selfie instead, if you must.'

Needless to say the little girls won me over, and I read them bedtime stories and joined in their games. They loved Lego (second-hand from eBay) which even I found very rewarding, and we built a replica of Tower Bridge, which I explained was in London like 'London Bridge'. They had never visited London, but Frank was arranging for them to have a proper winter Christmas there next year.

Zara, the elder one, asked me why I was a vegetarian.

'Well, when I was as young as you, I was encouraged to love animals, cuddle them, stroke them. I always wanted a dog or a cat, but my mum wouldn't let me, so I made do with my toy ones. And think of all the nursery rhymes we sing: *Mary Had a Little Lamb*; *Little Bo Peep*; *Baa Baa Black Sheep*, and all the cartoons like *Mickey Mouse*; *Donald Duck*; *Brer*

Rabbit, but we are encouraged to eat animal meat. It never made sense to me.'

'I've never eaten a mouse!' said Zara indignantly.

'And what about *24 blackbirds baked in a pie*? They get eaten,' said Zelda sternly.

'Anyway, what nursery rhyme is your favourite?' I asked.

Zelda sang:
'Hey diddle diddle,
The cat and the fiddle,
The cow jumped over the moon.
The little dog laughed,
To see such sport,
And the dish ran away with the spoon. '
We all laughed.

'Shall I tell you a joke?'

'Yes, pleeese!' they both screamed.

'Why did the chicken cross the road?'

'Don't know!' they chorused.

'To escape the battery farm.'

'What's a battery farm?'

'It's where most chickens have to live, where there's no room even to stand, and they're force-fed and killed for human consumption.'

Silence all round.

I spent hours walking on the empty pristine beaches with not a soul in sight. How different to those crowded, regimented beaches in Italy, full of matching-colour umbrellas and sunbeds for hire all pointing in the same direction, where you had to pay ludicrous amounts to sit on a deckchair!

Cousin Frank and his family took me on a few excursions to the centre of Melbourne, to restaurants, art galleries and museums. I even went to the cinema in Brighton one day on my own. Can't remember what I saw…

One evening we started chatting about our Italian family. I told Frank I had travelled to Calabria in the south where our grandmother Angela had hailed from.

'Some parts were pretty dodgy, but the scenery was beautiful… that deep blue sea, almost a navy-blue, the olive groves, those shepherd huts called *trulli* we passed on the way back up the Adriatic coast…'

'Remember Nonna Angela? She was a tough old bird. Must have been her Calabrian roots. She said her father was a fencing instructor, but Uncle Vince always said he worked for the mafia.'

'Yeah, I know. It's called *'Ndrangheta* – I can't even pronounce it – round those parts. Rosa said he became a bookkeeper.'

'Yeah, he did… I know he was kicked out of town and that's why he ended up in London.'

'What about the other side? Rosa never talked much about her mother's family. Well, she never talked about any of them. She didn't seem interested. But what about Alba? She married her second cousin, didn't she? Mungo and me briefly went to that village, what's it called? Torretta! Nothing much there. Apparently our ancestors were buried up at the old church, and their bones were then reburied at the new cemetery up the road from the new church but left unmarked. I think that's what someone in the village said. I couldn't find anything in the cemetery about our great-grandmother, what was her name now?'

'Ah, you mean Zaira.'

'I thought it was Raiza?'

'No, Zaira. All I know is Zaira left the village and eventually teamed up with some rich guy, Leonardo. He's our great-grandfather. She had illegitimate twins, a boy and a girl, but she gave up the son, Fabio, to Leonardo and his first wife. Then he died. Alba was their daughter. And eventually, Zaira and Leonardo married. I think they went back to live in Torretta.'

'So she had twins then, like your dad and Uncle Vince?'

'Yeah, my dad told me the whole story once. About all the sadness it caused. I mean, Fabio dying so young.'

'Rosa never told me anything. So what else do you know about Alba?'

'I know she was born in 1900 as it's easy to remember. Alba married Francesco (or Franco), our grandfather. His father, also Francesco, moved to London, and that's how the family business started really. He had a café in Clerkenwell, and then eventually my uncles set up three or four restaurants in the West End and one in the city. Well you know that. You worked for them for a while, didn't you?'

'Very briefly, I hated it. It was the one in Oxford Street (now a McDonald's, I seem to recollect). I remember fucking up the coffee machine the first day I was there and being told off for serving tiny ice-cream scoops. They were ten bob a shot which was a lot of money in those days. I never felt comfortable. Catering certainly wasn't in my blood, and I hated seeing all that meat.'

'You mean with being a vegetarian? What about here in Oz? You didn't seem squeamish at that barbie we went to yesterday.'

'I'm used to it, but I love the fruit and veg here. Really fresh and mainly organic too...'

'Well, depends where you shop...'

'Anyway, you were saying about Alba.'

'Yeah, apparently she married her second cousin, Franco, on the rebound. You know she studied to become a lawyer in Milan? Well she had a brief affair with a French student there. His name was Jacques and he was already engaged to be married. Luckily Jacques's parents were very kind to Alba when they discovered she was pregnant. They arranged for her to have the baby in France. She told everyone she was going on holiday to Toulouse with Zaira – this was 1919 I think – but she secretly had a baby son. With her consent, he was put up for adoption and raised by a French family. Ville… something.'

'So both Zaira and Alba had baby sons they gave up?'

'Yeah, and they both had twins. They say it runs in families.'

'What, giving up baby sons?'

'Well, yeah maybe that as well, but I meant having twins.'

'And what did Alba do after she gave up her son?'

'Zaira sent her to London to Uncle Franco's family, where I think she continued to study law for a while at Regent Street Polytechnic.'

'Did she actually qualify to practise law in England?'

'No, I don't think so. When she married Franco, our grandfather, she took care of the restaurant admin and did the accounts. Well, after it got too much for Nonna Angela.'

'Rosa said Alba helped Italian patients at a couple of London hospitals.'

'Yes, she used to translate for them, find their families accommodation, that kind of thing. And she even helped Italian young men avoid National Service in Italy by pleading their cases at the Home Office. She was very well-thought of by the London Italian community.'

'Did Nonno Francesco know she'd already had a baby?'

'Yeah, my dad said she confessed all to him when they got engaged. But he was so engrossed by the growing restaurant business he didn't seem to mind. He loved and admired her just the same. But something Alba wrote made me think that she definitely married him on the rebound and she never stopped loving Jacques. I found some letters after my dad died. She kept in contact with Jacques in France. It turned out he and his wife never had children, so Jacques kept a close eye on their son. His name was Jean, or something like that, and I believe he ended up in London too, but Alba never knew where…'

'What a story! My mind is really reeling!'

I started thinking about poor Grandmother Alba and the consequences of fate. She was obviously clever and ambitious, but never became the lawyer she wanted to be, thwarted by love, sex, the usual stuff. And I wonder if Grandfather Franco held her back. Would he have wanted a lawyer as a wife? I bet he encouraged her to help out with his business as a way of restraining her.

Next day Frank, Adele, Zara and Zelda took me on a trip to see the Apostles on the Great Ocean Road. We stayed overnight en route at Port Fairy. Frank and I couldn't stop making up silly innuendoes about its name. The little girls laughed along with us, having no idea what we were really saying. They kept shouting 'Fairy, fairy, fairy!' from the back seat.

We stayed in a smart apartment Frank had found online. Shame we only stayed there one night as Port Fairy looked interesting.

The flat was hot and stuffy when we first arrived.

'I hate this humidity,' said Frank, turning on the air-conditioning full-blast.

'You hate humility?' I asked.

'Ha ha! Do you mind air-conditioning?'

'Nah, not at all.'

We arrived at our destination the following day. The Apostles are limestone cliffs situated on the Great Ocean Road National Park, towering over the rough and raging Southern Ocean. Apparently the soft limestone was gradually eroded by the forces of nature and formed fragile but huge arches and rock islands left isolated from the shore.

'There were twelve in all, but now there are only eight,' Frank explained adding that the one called London Bridge had fallen and collapsed quite recently.

'London Bridge is falling down, falling down…' chimed in the little girls.

Frank told me a funny story about this last *Apostle*.

'A group of day trippers on a coach, including a man and his female work colleague who were having an affair and on an illicit rendezvous, were out on London Bridge when it collapsed and started falling into the sea. They all had to be winched off pdq by helicopter.'

'Wished off?'

'No, they were rescued by helicopter. Then their names were splashed over the local paper and their secret love was no secret any more,' said Frank.

New Zealand Encounter

I would have liked to have
A baby daughter
Who looked like me.
Like Narcissus I'm
Attracted to like images.
Some gays and lesbians
Even heterosexuals
Are magnets to
Similar-looking partners.
What about me?
Can I now be
Clarus Clarisse?
Genesis P Orridge for instance,
He had plastic surgery
Changing his features
To match his partner's.
Grayson Perry and Eddie Izzard,
Straight but transvestites…
Why not me?

After spending a couple of weeks with Cousin Frank, I flew
to Christchurch via Sydney and hired a small camper van at
the airport, ideal for one person. It was a budget deal for a
high top Ford and easy to drive, but alas not in wonderful
condition. It was silly of me because now I could have
afforded a more luxurious camper. Like Rosa, I was always so
careful with money. I couldn't change the habit of a lifetime.

I have never incurred any debts or held any savings until

now… I'm not used to being rich! And apparently the Crispin Bars were sold recently to some brewery, I think Franco said. I didn't receive anything from the sale, but I would have been embarrassed if I had. Although I bet Rosa would have appreciated her share. Uncle Vince's daughters, whom I was never close to, didn't contact me about the proceedings, although I did get an email from Uncle Franco's other son, my cousin Gianni (he too is single, but someone I have nothing in common with). He said that the sale had been very difficult and there was less money than expected. He added a PS saying if ever I needed anything to let him know, but he obviously knew Mungo had left me well provided-for, so not sure why he said this – guilt possibly.

I found a campsite, situated between Christchurch and the Banks Peninsular, not far from the airport. I bought a cheese sandwich at the jolly-looking café and then had a quick nap in the van. Although the van was old, the new sleeping bag was cosy and made of soft duck down, and the mattress converted from the back seats was surprisingly comfortable. I was exhausted after the flight. When I had stayed in Melbourne my jetlag had abated and the time difference hadn't affected me after the first few days, but I was now feeling pretty jaded. My trans-continental travels were finally catching up with me, and the weather in New Zealand wasn't great either. My plan was to make my way up to North Island, but first I was heading out to the western coast across Arthur's Pass. Later that afternoon, feeling more rested, I decided to go on a short jaunt to the sea at Lyttleton. The scenery was superb, and I was just starting to relax and enjoy myself when I came across a dark, bedraggled woman standing beside a Nissan X Trail. She had broken down and looked distraught. I stopped and asked if I could help.

'Can you please give me a lift into Christchurch? No,

actually, I've changed my mind. I want to go straight to the airport.'

'I can take you there if you wish.'

'Okay, that's very kind of you! Let me first ring the car hire company to come and pick this up. And I also need to cancel my booking at the hotel in Christchurch for tomorrow. When I tried just now I couldn't get through for some reason. Maybe I took the number down wrongly.'

'Look, I haven't got any fixed schedule. I can drop you at the airport and then go to the hotel tomorrow, if that's not too late. I haven't looked round the city centre yet.'

'Hey, it's really generous of you. Thank you so much.'

'No problem.'

She hopped into the passenger seat of the camper van. It was rather shabby and smelly, and I had meant to cover it in a towel. The plastic seat was torn, but she didn't notice. She flung all her belongings over the back. Not much, just a large canvas bag, an umbrella and a book…

'I'm Clarisse. What's your name?'

'Dee Crispin.'

'Oh like the *Crispin Bars* in London?'

'Yeah, they belonged to my uncles.'

'So are you from London too? I suppose the answer must be yes, judging by your accent.'

'Certainly am, Islington born and bred.'

She became animated.

'Hey, so was I! I lived at the Angel, near Camden Passage, the antiques market. What street did you live in?'

'Dorset Street.'

'That's where I lived! Hey, this is amazing…'

More than amazing, I was completely flabbergasted. I swallowed.

'I know who you are. You're Clara, aren't you? I called

you Clarrie.' She looked so different, so bedraggled, almost like a tramp.

'Never liked Clara, and Clarrie was what I was called at school. Hated it!'

'You lived opposite me. You're French, aren't you?'

'Well my mum and dad were. Delphine and Eugène.'

'Gene? Was he born in London?'

'Eugène. Well, yes he always said he was, but Delphine, my mother, said technically he was born in Toulouse. They moved to London when he was tiny and registered his birth in England so that he would have British citizenship. His parents wanted to start a new life. He never spoke much about his family in France.'

'I discovered very recently from my Australian cousin that my grandmother had a baby son in Toulouse. My great-grandmother, Zaira, packed her off to London pretty sharpish after that.'

'Gosh, this is extraordinary. I remember my dad mentioning someone called Raiza, but it could have been Zaira. We christened her Daisy.'

'Well, maybe we're cousins!'

I was joking, but the realisation slowly dawned on me that Eugène could be Zaira's grandson. Well, well, well. But did I really want to pursue this? It was all too much. We *were* related. Was this why I had always been obsessed by her? Some subconscious primeval knowledge… Yet although I had never harboured any intense sexual feelings towards her, I did have this mental picture of her standing in front of her window in a flimsy shirt showing her upturned bare breasts. She must have been around thirteen at the time.

Should I say anything? Maybe not…

It didn't take long to get to the airport. By this time I knew quite a few details about her life and she'd guessed I was deaf. The strange thing was she enunciated every word, speaking so clearly that I could hear her high tones perfectly well. It was men's voices that were more problematic.

She got out of the van, gathering everything up in a hurry. She had very little luggage. And that's when she must have left her journal behind. We promised to keep in touch and exchanged email addresses.

I didn't have much time to forge an impression of the parts of New Zealand I visited, but it seemed a warm, vibrant, modern place. New Zealand has changed rapidly over the past twenty years. There are over two hundred ethnic groups in Auckland, and it's considered more diverse than London or Sydney. Trade with Asia has turned New Zealand into a globalised economy, although some of its public services like health are quite basic. What I did notice was that Māori culture seemed to be flourishing here, compared to the Aboriginal one in Australia. I saw some wonderful Aborigine art in the Melbourne art galleries, but non-indigenous white collectors and galleries control most of it. Aborigines still live in dirty shacks and are more or less encouraged by the state to drink themselves stupid. The Māori of New Zealand were similarly treated badly and left with little land by the colonialists, but they have been more organised and effective in getting some redress. They pleaded for financial compensation and the re-establishment of their cultural identity. The New Zealand government have been reluctant to pay out huge sums, but the Māori fought strongly against this and eventually got their way, receiving large financial settlements. In fact, the process in New Zealand has been seen as an international example of how to resolve historic grievances. I also know that New Zealand was one of the first countries to give women the vote, although they took their lead from Britain when it came to legalising homosexuality.

The earthquake forced me to change my plans. I didn't want to be anywhere near the devastation it had created, so I headed north straight away. It took me three days to get to the ferry for North Island, staying at unmemorable campsites en route. After I'd visited Nelson, Wellington and Rotorua, I cut my trip short and flew from Auckland via Hong Kong back to London. And I certainly don't want to write a journal about it the way she did…

Settling Down

I am waiting for death
Or rather death waits for me.
I don't want to die.
How will the ending be?
Unbearable pain,
Lingering,
Gasping for breath.
Top myself rather than
Wait for it to get me.
Swallow tons of pills
Or make a public statement.
Douse my clothes in petrol,
Setting alight to myself.
Make the news.
But I never will.
Too squeamish
Like being a doctor.
Or a lawyer,
Meeting criminals,
Murderers,
Defending someone
You know is guilty.

When I got back to London, I tried to dismiss any thoughts about her and all the accidental discoveries that had occurred while I was away. My trip had been cut short because of the earthquake, but what a revelation it had been – an exploration of my identity, and more a psychological adventure rather than one of geography. Many of us are not who we think we are. Eugène, her father, for instance, was adopted, although at least he was still French, unlike me who grew up believing I was half-Polish! And many of us have obscure parentage. Eric Clapton from Cream – one of my favourite bands – he thought his grandparents were his parents and his mother his sister. There must be thousands of other examples.

I settled into the house in Holloway. I was lucky I didn't have to work any longer, but I really missed my car park attendant job. I had found it strangely fulfilling. You don't have to be rich to feel some satisfaction in life. My menial low-paid jobs didn't stop me from gaining 'educated' views. Working at Lincoln's Inn gave me intellectual wealth, and now I had financial wealth too.

Under the froth and false gaiety, and despite the hues of our skin, we are more equal than we seem. We can be healthy, wealthy and beautiful yet suffer illnesses, chronic and acute, mental preoccupations, stresses and depressions, lack of confidence or panic attacks. Success doesn't necessarily mean happiness. A road sweeper can enjoy his work. Brushing away litter gives satisfaction, metaphorically clearing away the rubbish in the soul. The soulless banker or businessman obsessed with profits has a bleak morality. Emptiness and despair exist in us all, despite the rung of the social ladder we have reached. All is precarious. All are damned.

I had the rooms decorated one by one, painting them all a brilliant white. I left the fittings in the kitchen and bathrooms as they were. Mungo had had them modernised in the eighties. The main kitchen is French-style with pine cupboards and dark-blue tiles. After I gave it a new coat of paint it looked fine. One of the bathrooms is avocado, but I don't care. I am hoping it will come back into fashion one day.

I am concentrating on my new-found interest in antiques. I have given up collecting art deco and fifties' china. Recently I became more interested in Victorian or Georgian stuff and collecting automata. I can afford them now. I have always been intrigued by brass marine instruments: sextants, compasses, ships' clocks and mechanical model ships. And when I visit art galleries I always love kinetic art. The modern examples of automata are fascinating because they don't try to hide their internal mechanisms. I enjoy looking at and admiring the inside workings rather than the external coverings such as in Victorian toys. The intricate combination of gears, wheels and wires, as well as the sounds they make, are what I admire. Most automata are hand-cranked. Some are driven by wind, water or a small electric motor. None of them incorporate electronics. They can use the simplest of materials and they work along the same lines as watermills, windmills or human-powered cranes. Yet in spite of my fascination and admiration of them, I have no interest in learning how they actually work.

And only yesterday in Hampstead I acquired a brass parallel ruler with moveable parts for plotting charts and a beautiful brass skeletal clock. It has six spoke wheels, two pillars with ornate scrolls and a hammer that pings a bell every hour.

Now I am also looking for unusual tea caddies. Tea was so expensive in the eighteenth century it had to be locked in a caddy. Only the wealthy upper classes could afford it. I drink tea all the time, mostly green or camomile. I take it for granted. I can't imagine keeping it under lock and key.

And I still write stories.

Antique Road Steal

Job last night in St John's Wood. Great swag. Silver candlesticks, cutlery, loads of serving dishes and platters, tea set, coffee service, all to be melted down. Paintings can be sold to Larry the dealer. China and ornaments can all be sold on eBay.

The best thing is a tea caddy, and I have an idea.

Put it on Flog It. I've always wanted to be on TV, now's my chance. Need a disguise, though. Don't want every tom, dick and harry of the trade recognising me. I know, I will dress up as a woman. My long hair is good, just need to add make-up (Sue can help). Need some of those earrings, what they called? Clip-ons, yeah, that's it. High heels might be a problem – never worn them in my life. Maybe wedge hills (I mean heels) would be better. Dress, no problem, get one from charity shop. Talking of charity shop, I can say I work for one. Which one though? Okay, what about Otosclerosis Society? Will they check? Doubt it. It's very obscure, no one on telly will know the name.

So how do I apply? Need to find out what local town they will be at next. Check it out on the net. Easy peasy. Norwich Castle Gallery. So head up there in a taxi and join the queue, dressed to kill. Some short geezer likes the tea caddy. Next thing I know I am at this table covered in blue felt talking to a huge fat geezer, like Hagrid in the Harry Potter films. Can't remember his name.

'Hello, what's your name?'

'I'm Hilda and I work in the Otosclerosis charity shop. Someone brought this in and I would like to find out more about it.'

The guy says:

'The tea caddy is a handsome fellow!'

I murmur approval.

'Georgian, inlaid satinwood in mahogany, twin compartment in sarcophagus form, the interior fitted with two tea caddies with hinged lids and a mixing bowl. Brass lion mask handles, raised on ball and claw feet, and shield escutcheon.'

He's getting excited. He says it's got George III's monogram on it.

'Very rare indeed!'

I say the money will go to the charity. Next thing I know I'm in front of the TV cameras talking to Paul or Mark, or that other geezer from Malvern, Phil? Yeah, that's who it is!

He estimates it at £200 – £300, reserve £180.

I say: 'Can't we make the estimate 200?'

He agrees, of course, and invites me to the auction at Diss in Norfolk. It takes ages, over six weeks, and I am getting very irritable. Will my plan still work?

Decide to have a full makeover. Luckily I'm not hairy, but have total dilapidation, I mean depilation, at local beauty salon and get great little dress and clip-on earrings from Norwich charity shop. Have to wear same wedge shoes cos I can't find anything else that would fit me.

It's nearly time to drive up to Diss, but I am ready: cool, calm and collected. When I arrive in Diss I'm sweating all over; even the fucking shoes are hot and stink like the inside of a whore's cunt. No, I can't say that; like the rotting innards of a garbage truck.

The lady auctioneer asks for a bid at 200. Agreed, then 220, 250, 300, 350, 400, 450, 500. Next thing I know it's 1,000 knicker.

Phew. What a doddle! Didn't think it would be so simple.

I could carry on doing this. It's great, it's addictive. As long as no one recognises me, or realises the Otosclerosis charity shop doesn't exist…

Afterword

I mislaid her email address somehow. I must have lost it in transit. It wasn't difficult to trace 'Clarisse Villeneuve' as she calls herself on Facebook. There were two: one in France was a '*stripteaseuse gogo danseuse*' without a photo! The other was her. I recognised her hair.

There was only one of me. I was still Dorek Wiadrowski. I called myself Dee Crispin only informally, not officially – yet.

I sent her a message and she replied almost instantly. We exchanged email addresses and I arranged to meet her in Nettlebury where she lived.

'Clarisse' lived in a modern flat in a converted Victorian malt store on the Dove river estuary. Nettlebury was a charming village with a little fountain and a stone swan at its centre. It was famous for its swans, and there were a few small industrial units on the Quay – *I wrote Key* – even some boats. Russian, she said. The swans' arrival was down to their attraction to the waste deposited into the river estuary from the maltings, one of which was still in operation.

When I handed back her journal, she didn't seem particularly grateful, only surprised that she had left it in my van. She had barely any recollection of the latter part of her journey. She said she had phoned her son at Christchurch airport, telling him her plans, and then waited about five hours for the next flight back to Heathrow.

'Thank goodness I got out when I did. I missed that dreadful earthquake.'

I told her how I had gone to Christchurch to find her hotel not that long after it happened. 'There must have been roadblocks or police warning people not to enter the worst-hit areas, but I never noticed any barriers and just drove in. It was like a war zone.'

'Maybe it was destiny that day that made my car break down and influenced me to return home…'

She looked much better, not so skinny and more neatly dressed than when I'd seen her in New Zealand. Her curly hair wasn't so wild but surrounded her face like a halo. She was still beautiful, but I couldn't say I had any feelings for her. She was no longer that little delicate china doll from Dorset Street with whom I had been so obsessed.

'Come and sit on the sofa here.'

She was in remission, she said, from breast cancer, but was having regular check-ups at Ipchester hospital. I suddenly realised that Colwich hospital was also nearby. That was where Victor Leach had worked.

Suddenly Clarisse got up to answer the door. I hadn't heard anything, but a tall, very attractive blonde woman came into the flat. I stood up.

'Hello, I'm Jill Jessop,' she said immediately, addressing me in a clear soprano voice and shaking my hand. Jill was Clarisse's best friend and neighbour. I gained the impression Jill wanted to check up on Clarisse and check me out too at the same time. She had a very friendly and charming manner. Clarisse was lucky to have her. Jill seemed to sense that we were having a serious conversation and didn't stay long. We made small talk and then polite goodbyes. I walked out onto Clarisse's balcony which had a marvellous view of the River Dove.

She called out to me:

'Blowing a gale out there?'

'No, it's not blowing a gale.'

'I said: "Lovely day out there." Never mind, now that

we're alone let's carry on with our chat. Sit down next to me. We have lots to talk about.'

I reiterated that we had once lived across the street from each other. Like her trip to New Zealand, she didn't seem to recall it very clearly.

'Dorset Street was so different when I was a baby. I used to be parked outside my house in my pram without anyone ever worrying about baby-snatchers! I have photos of me in my smart black Silver Cross pram playing with my plastic rattle and toys strung on elastic…'

'Oh yes, I remember those big prams. But I don't remember being left out in the street! Can you imagine parents doing that now? Social services would be called in!'

'Do you remember the bomb sites?'

'Oh yes, especially the one in front of St James Church.'

'Rosa and I always sang that song when we walked through it. "I love to go a wondering along the mountain track".'

'You mean a-wandering?'

'What? Yes, I always get wondering and wandering muddled.' And even when my hearing wasn't so bad, I often misunderstood song lyrics. Do you remember Herman's Hermits' *She's a must to avoid*? I always sang "She's a muscular boy" instead!'

'Yes, it's easy to mishear pop songs. Even after I realised it wasn't right, I always used to deliberately sing, "Beg steel a biro" for *Beg, steel or borrow* by the New Seekers!'

'I remember that song. I liked Judith Durham.'

'One thing I do remember about Dorset Street were the iron coal holes that led to the coal cellars in the pavements in front of our houses. How the mysterious soot-covered men heaved the heavy sacks of coal off their lorry and then swiftly poured the lumps of coal through the hole into the cellar. Very efficient, and avoided coal dust getting into the house…'

'What about your seventh birthday? That gigantic cracker you had delivered. I got a plastic sailing boat.'

'You were there?'

'Yes, with André, Stephen and Renzo.'

'Oh I remember Renzo, but I really can't remember you. Renzo did my mum's hair for a while.'

'He came to a sorry end.'

I was about to explain what a gory death he'd suffered, but she didn't seem very interested.

'I can't really recall many people from the street.'

'My mum was Rosa. She was friendly with your grandmother, Celeste. She adored her. She saved my life when I was a baby. I had pneumonia and was dying. Even though Rosa was a nurse, she froze and was too hysterical to know what to do.'

'Oh! I didn't realise that. But I do remember the doctors' house on the corner and the Polish church.'

'Well, I lived in the house where they had the Polish school.'

'Oh yes, I remember now,' she murmured.

'And what doctor did you used to see?'

'I hated that place. I never went unless my mum forced me. I remember a Doctor Linley. She was married to a very nasty man, also a doctor, but I can't recollect his name. He molested me once, but Delphine, my mother, wouldn't take it any further.

'I thought she was a lesbian… Rosa always said she was having a relationship with the receptionist.'

'Really? I don't think so. I remember her husband very clearly. My mum didn't take it any further because Dr Linley was married to him.'

'How odd, I didn't think she was married. We all have different recollections, different secrets, skeletons in the cupboard and all that…'

'Erm, I suppose we do. What about you?'

'Well, I did discover that my father wasn't my biological one. Rosa told me he was Polish and died soon after I was born. In fact he died two years before that. It seems I am a product of a liaison she had with a doctor. Strangely enough, somewhere near here in East Anglia. The odd thing is that I've always felt rather Polish.

'Yes, I suppose one could say you even look Polish.'

'Well, I'm not. I was named Dorek Wiadrowski, but my name should be Crespi (anglicised to Crispin) like my mother or Leach like my father. As I told you before when we first met, I go by Crispin these days.'

'Did you say Leach? I knew a Victor Leach here once. Not sure what has happened to him though. I can't bring myself to find out now, but I was obsessed with him for a while, really obsessed. It's difficult to explain.'

'I think I understand what you mean,' I muttered.

'He was a doctor at Colwich hospital. We didn't have an affair, but there was something between us, an intimate friendship if nothing else. Then it all went wrong. He suddenly stopped talking to me, saying he never wanted to see me again. It was just after I discovered I had breast cancer, and he was a *breast surgeon*! My faith in doctors has never been good (not after Dorset Street) but I went completely crazy. How could he, of all people, be so cold towards me when I had breast cancer?

'I've never admitted this to anyone before now, but one day I went to his office at the hospital in a strange dreamlike state. I wanted to hurt him physically, harm him. I picked up a medical instrument – a scalpel – lying on a trolley in a corridor and quickly unwrapped it. When I arrived at his office he had his back to me. It would have been so easy to stab him, but I didn't. I didn't even speak to him. I turned round and ran away, and never went back to that hospital ever again. I transferred to Ipchester and actually found a doctor there I was able to respect.'

I didn't know what to say. I decided not to mention that Victor Leach was actually my half-brother. Maybe she would try to knife me too.

This stuff about Victor, am I fantasising?

Is it unbelievable? Who can tell? Tell it like it is, or how you feel things, wish things?

I certainly don't want this. All this coincidence stuff. I want to walk away. I don't want these connections to her now.

'I have fantasies all the time. I sometimes can't remember if things actually happened or whether I make them up. I have this ongoing impulse to kill our useless political leaders,' I said, reassuringly.

'I know what you mean. I've often wondered why terminally ill people don't assassinate more politicians. I would've loved to have a pop at our career-politicians. But after my encounter with Victor, I realised I would never have the courage.'

'Me too. I had endless fantasies about the Mayor of London, *and* that twerp Berlusconi. My Italian uncles admired him. I could never understand it.'

'Me neither, such a horrid little man. In fact, in a way he reminded me of Victor: a combination of charm, vanity and testosterone – obviously chemically enhanced.'

'What did Victor look like?'

'He was typically tall, dark and handsome, not really like the diminutive Silvio.'

'Ah, he was dark.'

'Yes, well, actually he had grey hair, almost white. Why do you ask...?'

'No reason... Erm, I was going to say we're talking more now than we ever did when we lived opposite each other.'

You know I was obsessed with you when I lived in Dorset Street? I loved you, even wanted to be you. I know now that it was an illusion. I am incapable of real love. I don't want to love you, live with you, be you. My obsession with you is over...

'I hope you're not offended, but I really can't remember you. I do still have days when I have memory problems. In New Zealand when you found me in my broken down car, I was broken down too, both physically and mentally...'

'Well, you look much better now.'

'Thanks! I decided the trip to New Zealand wasn't the answer. I was losing my grip on reality. I needed to get back here, to my little flat. And I am resigned to the fact that if the cancer returns, I have done enough soul-searching. I can confront death.'

'What about your son?'

'He has his own life to lead. He has no need to worry about me.'

She asked me about my deafness. 'How do you cope, not hearing?'

'I manage. My hearing has deteriorated further over the years, but my digital hearing aids are pretty effective, although not perfect. I must admit that some people are quite dismissive when I tell them I'm deaf. They often say, "Oh, I am too!" They don't seem to differentiate between normal hearing loss caused by ageing and severe hearing loss, like mine, suffered by much younger people.

'Blind people are usually much more respected, except if you're David Blunkett! Poor chap. I always felt sorry for him, and I remember him saying once if you're blind you can't be a racist. He was at school with a blind girl from South Africa, and her fellow countrymen made a point of telling her who the people of colour were. Blindness is deemed a tragedy, and when blind people are out in public they are helped to cross roads, to get onto buses or tubes and so on. It's a much more "visible" disability than deafness. When I say I can't hear or understand, people treat me as if I'm stupid.

'In Italy, I tried hard to practise my Italian, but when I said "Non sento" or "non capisco bene" Italians invariably replied in English as they thought I couldn't speak any Italian. It got quite frustrating, but I suppose they wanted to practise their English too! And I also discovered that Italians have their hearing aids set differently to hear the Italian language compared to mine set to hear the English language...'

'You must feel lonely – or solitary.'

'I do, but you must get lonely too.'

'Yes, I do, but I have my books. I still enjoy films, and I write.'

'That's funny, so do I.'

'Oh, what do you write?'

'I'm actually writing the story of my life, about my family background, about obsessions, fantasies, politics...'

'Sounds interesting... and do I feature in it?'

'Of course. It was your journal that started me writing it.'

'Well, I feel flattered. And the other funny thing is that I did want to write an historical memoir about Raiza/Zaira, thinking she was French. I even started doing some research, but I got distracted and didn't get very far.'

'We could collaborate and write an historical novel jointly.'

'Ha ha! You know, I really feel I know you. It's a pity I

was such a stuck up little bitch when I lived in Dorset Street. We could have become good friends. Maybe our lives would have been very different. You could have visited us when we lived in France.'

'I'm planning a visit there, actually. Paris definitely, and then who knows? Maybe the South of France as well. I've always wanted to visit Matisse country.'

'Oh, we used to go to a friend's flat near Nice. There's a museum there full of his stuff, and then in Antibes there's the Picasso museum, and Vence is very interesting too, with the Matisse Chapel… Oh, I would love to show you all these things…'

'It's so weird after all these years, coming together like this, the coincidence of it all.'

'I love coincidences… tell me, have you ever had a girlfriend … or boyfriend for that matter?'

I laughed. 'No, I've never been interested in either sex. I sometimes wonder why not. I have never told anyone this before, but I did visit a prostitute once in Shepherd's Market, which was a complete disaster. After that I steered clear of sex stuff. I had a very emotional relationship with Rosa, my mother, and then I was very close to Mungo, who was my best friend until he died, but no real sexual relationship. I suppose you would say I'm asexual, and I'm comfortable with that now…

'The dating ritual was never an option for me. It never even occurred to me to ask anyone out. I didn't want to play the game, didn't want to fit in. I wasn't remotely interested in French kissing, love bites or fumblings like other boys. I was always surprised when boys at school assumed they would get married and have kids. Even Mungo Gerry, my best friend, would have loved to have children. Only my friend Damien and me said we didn't want to, but even Damien finally got married, in spite of having had the snip!'

'Well, children don't always turn out how you expect. They don't always end up looking after you when you're old. I'm sure many people have children for purely selfish reasons. As an only child, I could be demanding, manipulative, and my parents did spoil me. We tried not to spoil our son, Adam.'

'I wasn't spoilt, but I could easily have played the manipulative card with Rosa. I could smell her guilt about me, but at the same time she never let me forget that I had ruined her chances of settling down with another man.'

'Mmm, that's interesting. So many people's lives are influenced by sex, money or power, especially politicians' and celebrities'. I was always perplexed by my sexual longings as I was happy with my husband, Harry. But when he died I was pulled up short, like the momentum of a braking train or when a plane lands on the runway. I had to take stock and adjust. It took me a while, but now I've grown accustomed to my sexless passionless life. I like it. I have a routine which I always found hard before. I potter around. I go for long walks and see Jill and others in her social circle, although I enjoy my own company and I'm certainly no longer afraid of dying. I came to the conclusion a long time ago that we can't rely on other people. We all need love in our lives, but it's not necessarily a sexual love. Love can be about many things.'

'Well yes, I think people worry too much about love, sex, money, whatever. I've led a monotonous sexless life. I'm not really sure what love is and I have certainly never achieved any success, but I know my limitations. I accept them, am actually quite happy now. I have plans. I can use the money I've inherited to help other people. Love is about sharing.'

'What do you have in mind?'

'Not sure yet, still thinking about it. Possibly an asexual dating agency!' I joked.

'I was thinking, we could spend more time together. You

say your mother was a nurse. What about you? Would you be interested in nursing me when the time comes?'

'No, I don't think so.'

'Well, maybe it won't come to that. I was very stubborn about not having any chemo, but opinions have changed. In fact, there are types of chemo that don't have those dreadful side effects such as hair loss and so on now. It's radiotherapy that is currently being questioned for the risks it poses in terms of causing secondary cancers.'

'Oh, I didn't know that. Rosa always said chemo was poison.'

'The drug regime I'm on doesn't have any terrible side-affects. And I think the steroids are making me look quite plump...'

'Well, as I said, you definitely look healthier than when I saw you last.'

'Do you believe in euthanasia?'

'Yes I do.'

'Well, you could help me. You should be good at dispensing lethal injections.'

'Actually I must confess I'm squeamish – I hate blood. The irony was Rosa wanted me to be a doctor!'

'So did my mother,' added Clarisse. 'So you won't help me?'

'No, I don't think so... I don't think it would be right, not for me. But we can keep in touch. You know I don't like using the phone, but even though I couldn't get used to it at first, I'm now addicted to email.'

'So am I... Next time you visit me, I will take you to Crabness, further downstream on the estuary towards Sturwich. We can walk on the wonderful beach there. It's my favourite spot in the whole world.'

A pity we never did. When I looked back on this conversation it made me think about impossible coincidences in Victorian literature; the way they are used to drive a plot forward. I've been reading this novel *No Name* by Wilkie Collins, who was a friend of Dickens (another master of coincidence). Magdalen, the 18-year-old heroine, is no typical ideal of Victorian womanhood. When she is disinherited, she uses her physical charms to take revenge on the cousin whose father reduced her to poverty. She has been described as immoral, and like me, she has 'no name' and couldn't help being illegitimate. Rosa was extremely embittered when she inherited far less than her brothers from the family business. I know now that it was because she had me out of wedlock.

In the novel I particularly liked the comical Captain Wragge, the professional swindler who helps a disguised Magdalen to marry her cousin, Noel Vanstone, but I wasn't so sure about Captain Kirke. It was odd he fell in love with Magdalen after only one sighting, and then amazingly bumped into her in Camden. On the other hand I was pleased she was redeemed by his love at the end. The novel throws up many provocative questions about illegitimacy; good and evil natures; when it's right to act or be patient. Although it did make me wonder whether it was against the law to marry under a false name. I thought birth certificates had to be provided before a marriage, but perhaps not in those days. What amused me was when Noel Vanstone says: *"It's like a scene in a novel – it's like nothing in real life."*

Then Collins asks, in the guise of Miss Garth: *"Are there inbred forces of good and evil in all of us, deep down below the reach of mortal encouragement and mortal repression – hidden Good and hidden Evil, both alike at the mercy of the liberating opportunity and the sufficient temptation? Within these earthly limits, is earthly circumstance ever the key and*

*can no human vigilance warn us beforehand of the forces
imprisoned in ourselves which that key may unlock?"*

So I have two connections to Clarisse: one as a blood relative
via her father Eugène, and now Victor. The final cliché, the
pièce de résistance: Clarisse knew Victor, my half-brother.

It's mind-boggling, like the plot of an unbelievable
penny dreadful. I'm a character in a bad novel. I want to
disassociate myself from her, re-establish myself. Those times
I wasn't happy in my own skin and wanted to taste what it
would be like to be her instead, I don't feel this any more. For
the first time in my life I'm happy being me.

In the Holloway house there is an upstairs self-contained
flat where Yolanda was supposed to live in her retirement. She
never did live here. She died in her flat in Clerkenwell, not far
from her shop.

It needs a lick of paint and isn't by any means twenty
first-century modern, but I've had an idea. I've spruced the
flat up a bit and added some new IKEA furniture. Three single
beds, three wardrobes, sofa and two armchairs, six chairs,
table that will fit three people comfortably – three homeless
people. I have been to the local social security office and they
have agreed to advertise it. I have kept the advert short and
simple:

*CHEAP ACCOMMODATION IN HOLLOWAY
PLEASE TEXT ME ON 0788078807
INTERVIEWS IN TWO WEEKS*

I will choose the three that I think are most deserving. They
can live here rent-free and I will pay their council tax, but they

will have to see to their living expenses. I don't want to pay for everything and make them feel too inadequate…

It was Dino's son Jimmy who made me start thinking about the plight of the homeless. He runs a charity for homeless men out of St James Church in Islington. He's won awards and is in line for an OBE, Dino proudly told me.

I have now made donations to three churches when I don't even believe in God. Yet those three churches were like my family. One donation is to St Stan's Polish church – the priests obviously took pity on my mum when she got back to London and let her have that flat. Maybe they didn't know the full story and helped her out cos she'd been married to Piotr.

The other donations were to St James, the local Catholic church where we still play bowls, for their homeless charity, and St Paul's Italian church. Their club was my second home. The old priest there, Father Claudio, has devoted his life to helping drug-addicts and visiting them in prison or getting them off the London streets.

I've had a further idea. I was appalled to learn that metal spikes are being installed in various parts of London to prevent the homeless sleeping rough – like pigeon deterrents. 'Studs aren't the answer,' I thought…

The garden here is a good size for London. I am considering the purchase of a 'Wheelly'. A wheely, or wellie as I call it, is a portable and expandable shelter which can serve as a mobile home for homeless people. It's based on an Italian-design (of course!) and can be pushed around on its rubber-covered aluminium wheels, turned into a seat, and at night parked and expanded to make a sleeping area.

There's enough room for three wellies in this garden. Three young people have set up a company in London producing them. I have ordered three. They are arriving tomorrow.

I am now in discussions about investing in their

company. I want to achieve something, be more positive, get more involved, get off my apolitical fence. Although I get annoyed with politicians and joke about what I would do if I were prime minister, I am no activist and have never been involved in a political party. I don't even sign petitions. Do politicians ever read them? I went on that one demonstration – an anti-vivisection protest at a lab in Herts, but I got manhandled by a policeman which really put me off. I was just standing there innocently holding my banner and he grabbed hold of me and told me to move on. I went to a Labour party meeting once, but couldn't bear the protocol, points of order, verbose language, self-satisfied and self-important utterings or mutterings of everyone there. When I was young I was very anti-blood sports: fox hunting, hare coursing, even greyhound racing, and I certainly didn't believe in experimenting on animals. I certainly still don't believe in vivisection. Experiments for make-up products are still forced into animals eyes, which can result in their eyes closing up. If the product doesn't have this terrible effect, they are continually forced into animals' eyes and pronounced 'safe'.

As Wilkie Collins said in his novel *Heart and Science*: *"What proof [is] there that the effect of a poison on an animal may be trusted to inform us, with certainty, of the effect of the same poison on a man. To quote two instances only which justify doubt—and to take birds this time, by way of a change—a pigeon will swallow opium enough to kill a man, and will not be in the least affected by it; and parsley, which is an innocent herb in the stomach of a human being, is deadly poison to a parrot..."*

But I've never been a member of the Animal Liberation Front. To join you need to have a commitment to action. Support is not enough. That's why I'm not a member; too scared to commit a crime and get arrested... And as time goes on, the more I realise my fellow human beings are just as important.

Helping the homeless is the least I can do. I have been extremely lucky to have always had a roof over my head. I could have slithered down that slippery slope into debt if I hadn't had the help of family and then Mungo. It always made me angry that Thatcher made selling off council housing something to welcome. Monies received on sales should have been invested in new house-building schemes, more housing cooperatives and public/private joint ventures. The 'bedroom tax' is obviously a vast mistake and has forced people into rent arrears. They have been victimised and can't downsize because there are so few smaller properties. Why can't the government admit they made a mistake and repeal this ridiculous policy?

I occasionally expressed my political views on the online *Guardian* comments pages but the readers who responded to my innocuous suggestions were so rude and reactionary I stopped writing. I couldn't understand why those of a right-wing persuasion would read such a lefty newspaper. But even newspapers like *The Guardian*, as all the other media, have been dumbed down, and there is an absence of proper political analysis these days.

Somehow the local press have got hold of the Wellie story and they want to interview me next week – fame at last! The woman who emailed me also mentioned a *Mature Male* fashion shoot. She wants to know if I would be interested in appearing with nine other elderly men, including Jon Snow, in their weekend magazine. Blimey!

Postscript

My name is Clarus Crispin. I have grown my wavy white hair even longer. I wear baggy trousers, long brightly-coloured kaftans or floral shirts and beads. I feel closer to Clarisse now, closer than I can admit. No longer angry with her for our recently discovered connections. She asked for me – on the telephone. I knew it was serious. Neither of us likes the telephone for different reasons. I answered her call with trepidation, but I recognised her clear elocution-trained tones immediately. She wants me to visit her at the hospice.

Will I now tell her that I'm the first cousin she never had? She'd like that. And Victor, will I tell her that he is my half-brother? Perhaps, perhaps not. I haven't decided. Toss a coin, pull petals from a daisy. It might be too much for her. I will hold her hand, that will be enough.

I have a picture of her in Colwich hospice. She's in a semi-comatose state. I don't tell her about Victor. Does it really matter? I never knew him, or my father. I don't want to know them, absent fathers, dominant mothers. Is this why I'm the way I am, ungrounded, fantasising about her and living a dream life? Last time I saw her, her puzzled owl-round pale-blue eyes clouded, the dementia silently creeping up on her, I realised it was better she was approaching the end. And would she have understood what I was saying about Victor, that we were brothers? My obsession is finally buried with her, or rather, cremated. Some weird priest called Father Gabriel conducted the ecumenical service, half Catholic, half Anglican. He looked like the prophet Isaiah. Her son, whose name I didn't catch, scattered her ashes on Crabness beach at low tide. It is a magical place. Secluded and unspoilt, pervaded by that smell of mud, seaweed and salt water I have always loved. Quaint beach huts are dotted along the sprawling sands or set up in the cliffs in the places where they haven't eroded.

And now she's dead I regret not getting a chance to tell her I loved her. I never told anyone that. I remember that Sunday mass at St Stan's; she must have been thirteen, or even younger. She was so beautiful, like a Renaissance princess. She came through the heavy doors and tripped on the faded blue worn, torn cord matting covering the stone-flagged floor. She fell flat on her face, then pulled herself up in as dignified a manner as possible, beetroot red with embarrassment. I tried to talk to her after the mass, but she was either too shy or too stuck-up. I saw her some Sundays after that, but she always left hurriedly and never lingered, so I could never say hello.

How often do we ask ourselves: why am I me? Why aren't I someone else? Could I have been her? No, I think not. I am unique. Even our ear bones, like our fingerprints, are different. I couldn't be her. An identical twin could pretend, not me. And writing this book has made me comfortable in my own skin. Somehow I have found some inner peace.

I knew I would never find a publisher for my ravings and rantings, but that I could publish it myself. And I did, just for the hell of it. It wasn't that difficult. I could never have done this by traditional means, so thank you, *Tread Self-Publishing* and *FoolProof Designs*.

People may not read it; may not listen to what I have to say, but I've done it, that's what counts…

Note on Otosclerosis

The exact cause of otosclerosis is not fully understood. Genetic factors are involved, so the condition often (but not always) runs in families. Other factors thought to play a role include viral infections, in particular infection with the measles virus as otosclerosis appears to be less common amongst people who have been vaccinated against measles. It has also been suggested that otosclerosis may be affected by hormonal changes, or that it may be a form of autoimmune condition in which the body's defence mechanisms attack the body's own tissues.

In someone with normal hearing, the sound passes from the tympanic membrane (ear drum) to three small bones, or ossicles, which transmit the sound to the inner ear, or cochlea. The stapes, or stirrup bone, is the innermost of these ossicles. It is the smallest bone in the body and sits in a hole or 'window' into the cochlea. It is free to vibrate within the window, allowing transmission of sound. In otosclerosis the bone around the base of the stapes becomes thickened and eventually fuses with the bone of the cochlea. This reduces normal sound transmission, resulting in a conductive deafness. In the early stages of otosclerosis, the cochlea and the nerve for hearing are not affected, though eventually they can be.

Both ears may be affected, although in men it is more common for one ear to be worse. Untreated, the deafness gradually worsens, and in a small percentage of people it can cause profound hearing loss. Other symptoms of otosclerosis can include tinnitus and balance problems. Otosclerosis tends to affect the low frequencies more than the high frequencies. Pain is not usually a symptom.

Unfortunately there is no such organisation as the Otosclerosis Society.

For more information about asexualitiy, see Aven (Asexuality Visibility and Education Network) www.asexuality.org and www.platonicpartners.co.uk

ND - #0270 - 270225 - C0 - 216/138/15 - PB - 9780993010606 - Matt Lamination